They were just doing each other a favor, Jannes told himself sternly.

There was absolutely no reason to feel hesitant about agreeing to keep Lara company at her sister's wedding and then take her as his plus-one to an awards ceremony. They had eaten dinner together plenty of times. Been out drinking. Dancing together. This wouldn't be any different really.

And they'd both been very clear that this didn't change anything between them. They had been friends for three years and never even set a toe over the line between friendship and something more.

Because Lara was special and he was a mess, and she deserved so much more than that.

Dear Reader,

Lara and Jannes's story was written deep in the 2020 lockdown, when I could only dream of mooching around London markets, attending fancy parties and taking weekend trips to the seaside. I poured all my need for escapism into their story, and I hope that—if you need to—*From Best Friend to Fiancée* will help you escape for a few hours, too.

With love,

Ellie Darkins

From Best Friend to Fiancée

Ellie Darkins

Recycling programs
for this product may
not exist in your area.

ISBN-13: 978-1-335-56705-5

From Best Friend to Fiancée

Harlequin Enterprises ULC
22 Adelaide St. West, 40th Floor
Toronto, Ontario M5H 4E3, Canada
www.Harlequin.com

Printed in U.S.A.

Ellie Darkins spent her formative years devouring romance novels, and after completing her English degree decided to make a living from her love of books. As a writer and editor, she finds her work now entails dreaming up romantic proposals, hot dates with alpha males and trips to the past with dashing heroes. When she's not working, she can usually be found running around after her toddler, volunteering at her local library or escaping all the above with a good book and a vanilla latte.

Books by Ellie Darkins

Harlequin Romance

Newborn on Her Doorstep
Holiday with the Mystery Italian
Falling for the Rebel Princess
Conveniently Engaged to the Boss
Surprise Baby for the Heir
Falling Again for Her Island Fling
Reunited by the Tycoon's Twins
Snowbound at the Manor

Visit the Author Profile page at Harlequin.com.

This is for everyone who has called, texted, tweeted, messaged, sent cards, sent flowers and delivered milk to my door. This year has been a test of endurance for us all, but I've never felt more loved or supported by friends, family and complete strangers. Thank you all.

Praise for
Ellie Darkins

"All in all, this is another enjoyable, heartfelt, emotional romance from Ellie Darkins with characters you care about, and look forward to following their journey throughout the book. A thoroughly enjoyable story...which will leave you smiling, and perhaps crying a few happy tears along the way. An excellent read."

—*Goodreads* on *Falling Again for Her Island Fling*

CHAPTER ONE

'WHO KNEW THAT you were such a stud?' Lara said, eyeing Jannes over the top of the magazine.

'You know there's not a truthful word in the whole article, don't you?' her best friend replied with an eye roll and a withering look. He pulled the magazine back from her and pushed her towards one of the food stalls at Broadway Market. They'd met at the corner opposite London Fields, the same as they did every weekend he was in London, catching up on everything they'd been up to in the weeks that he'd been in Harbourside, the coastal town where his yacht club was located, or away sailing. That was the price you paid for your best friend being a professional athlete, she supposed. If he was going to keep winning these round-the-world races and breaking records left, right and centre, she was going to miss him while he was doing it.

But at least she got to see his face in the papers while he was away. Even if he wasn't very happy about it. She smirked at Jannes. 'At least they spelt your name right.'

He groaned. 'This isn't funny, Lara. All the sponsors we were lining up for the next transatlantic record attempt are freaking out. If they drop me because of this, then my plans will be down the toilet.'

She gave his arm a comforting squeeze and then bought him dhal and samosas from one of the stalls at Broadway Market, and crossed back over the road to eat in the park, spreading out her jacket on the grass as a make-shift picnic blanket. It felt like months since she had had the sun on her face. The winter had been long and hard, with an epic blizzard thrown in for good measure. But this morning she had woken up to spring. Her coat cupboard was still scattered with hats and scarves, but she'd left the house in just a sweater and a light jacket for the first time since September. London was glorious like this, and the whole of Hackney seemed to have a smile on their face.

She knew that her social feeds were going to be flooded with sunshiny pictures and iced coffees and spring flowers, and could hardly wait to launch her own spring theme. She made a mental note to take some pictures in the park before they headed back to her apartment. As an influencer, half her life was lived online, and the other half was spent studying for her MBA and launching her consultancy business, to help others achieve the success that she had found in building her little online community.

She took one look at Jannes, though, and stopped grinning. 'I'm sorry, Jannes. I don't know why they would make stuff up like this.'

He shook his head, looking again at the magazine. 'I went on, like, four dates this year. None of which went particularly well. And they've gathered every paparazzi photo that can possibly make me look like I'm with a girl and made me look like some sort of Casanova. I sneeze in a woman's general direction and all of a sudden I'm cheating with her on my other non-existent girlfriend.'

He said that as if she wasn't hyperaware of every date he had been on. As if she hadn't hung off his every word and nearly killed herself feigning nonchalance every time he had mentioned another woman's name. Really, sometimes it was exhausting loving Jannes as a friend the way she did, and him being beautiful, the way that he was. And knowing that under different circumstances—if she were someone different, someone less broken—that this could really be…something. But she was broken. And she wasn't someone different. And if she and Jannes tried turning this friendship into anything more then she knew that she would hurt him and lose him, and she just couldn't risk that. So she changed the subject, as she always did. Lightened the tone and tried to pretend that it didn't hurt. You'd think after three years of this, it would be easier.

'Or, you know,' she said, aiming light and hoping that her voice didn't shake. 'You've got your arm around a girl wearing a bikini…'

He hit her playfully on the arm with the magazine and she figured she'd got away with it. 'Oh, my God, I'd gone for a swim!' he protested. 'This is what I'm talking about. She slipped and I caught her. I probably saved her a concussion, but according to this we had a torrid three-day affair.' His voice sounded a little strained, and he was avoiding eye contact. Was he embarrassed about the picture? she wondered. Or was he in tune with her on this, as he was on just about anything else? Did he feel them drawing together every time that she did? Was he fighting as hard as she was?

'She does look a little dazed,' Lara observed, looking at the girl in the photo and accidentally dripping raita on her face.

Jannes shoved her with his foot. 'You're meant to be on my side.'

'Of course I'm on your side,' she told him gently. 'Tell me what I can do to help.'

'How are you with crisis PR?' he asked, a note of tension in his voice that she couldn't account for.

Lara smiled, after just a fraction of a hesitation. 'I don't know. I've never tried it, but I'll probably be excellent. What are you thinking?'

He shifted a little uncomfortably. 'Well, I had an idea. It was something my grandmother said, actually. The thing is, I have an awards thing in a couple of weeks, and it could be a good chance to present a new image. And I thought if you came with me, it might…change the narrative.'

'Explain,' Lara said, creasing her forehead as she listened to him.

'Well, people know that we're friends. We've been photographed together before. If we went together, and made it look like we were together, it would make me seem more…settled. Less…'

'Man slutty?'

He barked a laugh——she loved that. Loved that she could take him by surprise and make him lose control for a second. 'Well. Yes. You have this thing that makes people love you. I could do with a pinch of that.'

She frowned, thinking. 'I don't know, Jannes. It feels a little…weird. You're my best friend, and nothing more, and we've always been very clear about that. With each other. With everyone else. I'm worried that if we start bending the truth about that, there'll be a grey area, you know?'

'I know,' he said. 'And I agree. You know how much you mean to me, and I don't want to do anything that would risk that. But… Lara, I cannot lose this sponsorship. If I don't attempt the speed record this year—I don't know if I'll be able to do it again. And I can't think of another way to turn things around as quickly. And we know what we are, right? We know where we stand. That doesn't change.'

She thought about what he'd said while she ate. 'Why don't you take your grandmother?' she asked at last, thinking aloud, avoiding the proposal he'd put to her until she had thought about it some more. Maybe there was some other way out of this that didn't involve her examining her feelings for him quite so closely.

'You think I could trust Mormor near a TV camera?' Jannes said with a laugh. 'She'd be rampaging on my behalf. It was her idea that I ask you.'

Lara nodded. 'That's a good point. I love it when Mormor rampages.'

'Which is why it always terrifies me when you two are in a room together.'

She should agree to it, of course. She shouldn't even have to think about it. Jannes was one of her closest friends and, much as she would do just about anything to help him if he was in trouble, this was just…a little close to the bone. Because she was pretty sure that Jannes had been as determined as she had over the years to ensure that their friendship had never been in danger of being mistaken for more. And they'd never spoken about it, but she was pretty sure it was a battle that was being fought by both of them.

Jannes was a great guy. Certainly the best one that she knew. And Lara had a thing about nice guys—she didn't date them. What was the point when they got attached and she got attached and then they both got hurt? It hadn't taken her long into her twenties for her to realise that she was really bad at relationships. She'd freaked out the few times that things had been going well, and it had become clear that she wasn't cut out for making things serious.

Looking back, she knew exactly what the problem was—there was something wrong with her. When her father had walked out on her—for the other family he'd kept hidden from her her whole life—something inside her had broken. She wasn't sure what part it was, but somewhere along the line between dating and liking and loving, something was just…off. She was off. She tried to love and she couldn't, so she pushed boys away before she could hurt them. She wouldn't hurt Jannes. It was just unthinkable. Which was why she'd been keeping him firmly in the safe zone since the day that she had met him.

But he needed her, and she'd never been able to resist it when Jannes needed her. Eventually, she gave him her answer.

'Fine, I'll be your plus one,' she said. 'And I'll pretend to be your girlfriend. But we don't let this change anything between us, right? Everything stays the same. I don't want things to be confusing—I love you and you know that, but as friends and nothing more. I don't want anything to change.'

He nodded firmly, which gave her a little bit of confidence that this was all going to be fine, even if her gut was telling her something different. 'I know; I understand and I feel the same. This is all just for show. It doesn't change anything.'

'Good.' She let out a breath, let the tension drain from her shoulders. And then an idea struck.

'Hey, you know it's Pip's wedding next weekend? Will you come with me? If we're going to pretend to date, it'd be weird if you didn't, right?' If they were doing it once, what harm could it do to make it twice?

Her sister—her half-sister—had sent the invitation months ago, and she hadn't been able to say no, not when Pip had uninvited their father so that Lara wouldn't have to see him. She'd ignored the event in her calendar, hoping that something would come up that would mean she could get out of going. But nothing had and she'd been dreading it, but this could be perfect. She took a deep breath. 'I can't not go and I'm dreading it. I was going to just tough it out but… I'm wavering. So just do me a favour and hold my hand for a few hours?' He'd just told her that he wanted her to do practically the same thing for him, so it could hardly be a big deal.

'You know you could just find a nice boy to take you?' Jannes said at last.

Lara rolled her eyes. 'Ew, no thanks.'

Jannes laughed. 'Did you say *ew*? Are you twelve?'

'No, I'm thirty-one, very busy running a business where I'm expected to be available twenty-four-seven and can't be arsed filtering through all the douchebags in London to find the one decent guy left. So you'll have to do.' Which were all perfectly valid reasons for her not to date. And all true. But Jannes didn't need to know that they weren't the whole truth. That she didn't see the point in dating, when everything always ended in tears. And she didn't like doing that to people, least of all someone who she actually liked.

Jannes smiled, so broadly that it almost annoyed her. 'Ah, so you're going to convince me with flattery.'

'I'd ask Jess—' great friend, but also newly married '—but she's up in Yorkshire being deliciously loved-up with Rufus. For once you're not on a boat somewhere, you just asked me for a massive favour and I promise to buy you loads of booze if you say yes.'

He caved. 'Fine. Yes. You're very persuasive. But I don't get why you're dreading it,' he added, because he knew nothing about anything.

'You've never been a single woman in your thirties, have you, Jannes?' Lara said, giving him the most condescending look that she could muster. 'I can't be doing with everyone asking me when I'm going to find a nice young man and settle down.'

She felt a release of tension that she hadn't

known she was carrying when Jannes agreed to go with her. At a regular party, she would show up solo without giving it a second thought. But this was family, and her family was…complicated. Her half-sister was getting married, and had invited Lara to the big day. And when she said invited, she actually meant insisted, tearfully, on how much she wanted Lara to be there, and when she'd said that she wasn't sure it was a good idea…

That was when Pip, and her mother, and Lara's mother to boot, had suggested that maybe she needed to see someone about her issues with her family. That perhaps they could go to therapy. Family therapy, all of them together, and maybe even ask her father to go along too. She was practically sick at the thought. She had to do a better job of holding it together around them, or she was going to be subjected to that torture. Because how could she say no to Pip or her family, when they had taken her in when her world was falling apart?

She had no choice but to go to this wedding and convince them all that she was perfectly fine. There was no way that she was going to choose to do that either sober or alone.

'Fine, I'll come,' Jannes said, giving her a smile that crinkled his eyes. 'But are you sure that the whole pretending to be your boyfriend thing is necessary? I could come just as your friend. I mean, the best man might be hot. I don't want to cramp your style.'

'If he is, I'll drop you in a heartbeat, don't worry,' Lara said with a smile. 'It's just so that I don't have to spend the whole day defending my single lifestyle. You know they're all going to be talking behind my back anyway.'

He gave her one of those sympathetic looks that she hated. 'Jannes. Cut it out.'

It was only because he looked suitably remorseful that she decided at the last minute not to throw the chickpea she'd been threatening him with. 'Thank you,' she said. 'It'll be very romantic. Kidding,' she added, swatting him in the chest when his face went kind of grey. 'I'm kidding. Don't freak out.'

'I didn't freak out,' Jannes said, pulling himself up a little straighter.

Lara snorted. 'You so did. And one of these days we're going to talk about your rampant fear of commitment. But not until I'm done with you.'

'It's hard to know if that's a threat or not,' he said, narrowing his eyes.

'It's absolutely a threat.'

'Fine, we'll deal with my commitment issues when you're ready to talk about yours too.'

Pfft. What was the point of having a fake boyfriend instead of a real one if it didn't get you out of talking about your commitment issues? Besides, those commitment issues had been doing them both a favour ever since they'd met. You didn't meet a man as pretty as Jannes—and if anyone doubted a man could be pretty, she'd simply produce him as evidence—without being ever so slightly tempted to know what it would be like to get naked and sweaty with him, just the once. Besides, he was a nice boy, and she was a disaster with nice boys. She wasn't consigning Jannes to the 'do not drunk dial' group in her phone over a couple of nights of fun and then a major freak-out on her part. Or his, for that matter.

It wasn't worth losing him over an orgasm or two. However tempting he looked.

She could manage those all by herself.

No, she'd learned just not to think of him

like that. It hadn't been easy at first, what with the cheekbones and the muscles. The lithe hips and blond hair and the general wholesome Swedishness of him. But Lara was more than just her libido. And Jannes was more to her than just a pretty face.

They were just doing each other a favour, Jannes told himself sternly. There was absolutely no reason to feel hesitant about agreeing to keep Lara company at her sister's wedding and then take her as his plus one to an awards ceremony. They had eaten dinner together plenty of times. Been out drinking. Dancing together. This wouldn't be any different really.

And they'd both been very clear that this didn't change anything between them. They had been friends for three years and never even set a toe over the line between friendship and something more. Because Lara was special and he was a mess, and she deserved so much more than that.

He hadn't always felt this way about relationships. There'd been a time in his early twenties that he'd wanted it all. Someone to love. To settle down. And every time that he'd tried, the fear had started to creep in. The closer he got to someone, the darker the shadow hanging over him, waiting for the moment that they'd inevitably leave him.

He at least had the advantage of knowing what he was afraid of. He'd been left behind so many times that the scars that it had caused were etched deep into his soul. Every time he'd watched his parents drive away from his boarding school, the wound had gone a little deeper, past the point where it physically hurt to the place where it broke down who he was.

That feeling when they'd walked out of the door and he'd watched their car drive away was something he'd sworn he wasn't going to allow to happen again. And the safest way to ensure that he didn't have to watch anyone leave? He didn't exactly need a degree in psychology to see the connection with a career that kept him constantly on the move. He'd taken up sailing at boarding school; it needed enough concentration that he couldn't think about much else while he was out on the water. And schoolboy competitions had led to life as a professional competitive yachtsman.

Maybe that was where the playboy image

had come from. The few attempts that he'd made at relationships had fizzled out over the months that he'd been away sailing. The people he'd been with hadn't liked being left any more than he had, and he hadn't liked the thought that he had been hurting someone as much as he had been hurt. So it had made sense to stop trying to make relationships work. There had been a few short-term things over the years, when he'd been in one place long enough to see someone for more than a night or two. But knowing a relationship wouldn't last put a dampener on things, stopping them from ever really taking off.

And when it came to Lara, there was just no way that he could start something with her, knowing how it would end. Knowing that he would hurt her. Which was why it was so important that if they were going to do this thing, they were completely open with one another. There wasn't room in this for misunderstandings. They had to trust one another.

'There's something we should talk about,' he said, wondering whether she could hear his doubt in his voice. He had planned to bring this up nearer the time, but if they were going

to go to Pip's wedding next weekend, they
were going to have to do this now.

'Everyone knows that we're friends. We've
been photographed plenty of times before; it
never stopped me dating other people. If we
want people to believe that things are different now, that we're together, then we're going
to have to look as if we're...together.'

'Meaning?'

'Well, we should probably agree to some of
the details before the wedding,' Jannes said,
'if we're telling people that I'm your boyfriend. Get our stories straight. Agree to our
ground rules.'

'For goodness sake, Jannes. We don't need
a contract. I'm not going to make you sleep
with me!' Lara said with a laugh.

He frowned before he could catch himself. He hadn't thought for a second that she
would, but was the prospect really so appall-
ing? He certainly didn't think so. In fact, if
Lara wasn't one of his best friends, he'd find
the thought of it rather...appealing. But she
was one of his best friends. She was one of
the people that he liked best in the world, and
that meant that he wasn't willing to risk hav-

ing her in his life over something physical and meaningless. They were more than that.

'I know that,' he said. 'That's not what I meant at all.'

She laughed, and he wondered whether he was blushing. He felt as if he was probably blushing. 'Ha, well, I guess dating me is going to be full of surprises.'

He shook his head. 'I'm not sure I'm able to…' How were they meant to have a serious conversation when she was so…disarming? He needed to tiptoe through this, and she was forcing him to leap.

'You wanted to get our stories straight,' Lara said, changing the subject. 'How complicated are you expecting our origin story to be?'

He shrugged, going with it, because what else could he do in the face of Lara's enthusiasm? He'd never been able to resist. 'I don't know. Not complicated, but if someone asks us where we went on our first date and we don't know, then the gig is going to be up.'

'Fine.' Lara crossed her legs and rested her elbows on her knees, leaning closer to him and fixing him with a mischievous look. 'Where do you want me to take you on our imaginary first date? Knock yourself out. Choose something fancy—I'm buying.'

He raised one eyebrow. 'So generous.'

'Well, I like to treat you like a princess,' she said, lifting one corner of her lips in a smile. 'You deserve it, baby.'

'Baby?' He gave her a strong look, trying not to laugh.

'Babe?' she suggested.

He shook his head. 'Absolutely not.'

'Darling? Sweetheart? Cutie pie?'

He was in so much trouble.

She turned and pressed an impulsive kiss on his cheek and he just knew that that smirk on her face was because he was blushing.

'So. There are other things that we need to talk about if our story is that we're together now. Not just friends. Like kissing,' he said, blurting the words out as he rubbed at his cheek, his fingers catching where her lip balm had left a shimmer of stickiness. 'We might have to do that. Would it look weird if we didn't?'

'It might do,' she agreed. 'If you need the story in the press to be that we're together now, they're going to want the pictures to go with it.'

He nodded slowly. That was what he had been thinking too. But kissing Lara... That would... It wouldn't just be a kiss. Would it? With his best friend? Maybe it could be. Maybe he was making all this just too damn complicated. They had just said that this wouldn't change anything about who they were to each other, after all. If the kissing wasn't real, it shouldn't be a big deal. 'Do you think we should...practice?' he asked.

She narrowed her eyes at him. 'How complicated do you normally make it?'

He pulled her to her feet, took a step towards her, bringing his body right in front of her so she had to tilt her head back to look him in the eye.

'Depends on the occasion. And who I'm kissing. But the last thing we want is a picture of us that makes it obvious we're faking this. If we feel awkward just talking about it between ourselves, how's that going to come across to anyone else?'

'That's a fair point,' she said, not moving any closer. 'So...' she said, hesitating slightly. Up this close, standing like this, she felt less like laughing. This was serious. Suddenly, as Jannes's tongue moistened his lower lip, she felt her teeth close around her own. She wasn't sure this was a good idea. Was equally sure that it didn't matter because she was going to do it anyway.

This was Jannes. Lovely, safe Jannes. Who would never hurt her, who couldn't hurt her, because they both knew exactly what this was: fake. And she couldn't hurt him, because faking this was his idea.

'All right, then,' she said, eyes fixed on his mouth, noticing for the first time how the light caught at the top of his cupid's bow, the touch of shadow below the fullness of his bottom lip.

He tucked her hair behind her ear, a light, friendly touch. Something that wouldn't ordinarily make her pulse stutter, make her draw in a breath and hold it, not sure when she'd get a chance for another. His fingers lingered behind the curve of her ear, hit a sensitive spot that made her bite down harder on her lip.

This was nothing. It was friendly. They were friends and this was a friendly kiss. Not even that. Just a practice run at a friendly kiss.

Until his hand threaded in her hair, tightening at the nape, and she found herself swaying into him. She put a hand out to steady herself—felt considerably less steady when it landed on Jannes's hip. She held on, fingers curling round the jut of his hipbone, and let her eyes leave his mouth to flick up to his eyes. His lids were half-lowered, long blond lashes catching sunlight, glinting gold at the tips. Pupils blown wide, deep blue irises barely visible.

'Jannes...' She had just managed the word when his head lowered, eyes sweeping shut, tongue darting to moisten his lips one more time.

For a second she couldn't move, could only absorb the soft drag of his lips over hers, until instinct took over and she started to move against him.

Her other hand found his waist and she lifted to her tiptoes, hands anchored on Jannes, using him to push herself closer, higher.

Her tongue flickered out, tasting his bottom lip, just as Jannes's hand in her hair tilted her, changing the angle so their noses brushed together. So that when he bowed his body closer to hers, her head tipped back and her mouth opened, deepening the kiss and letting out a low moan as his tongue stroked along hers, hot and confident in her mouth.

His other arm was a vice in the small of her back, pinning her to his body with the strength of muscles built and honed as a professional athlete.

This was a *kiss*.

Her brain scrambled to catch up while her body took liberties. One hand in Jannes's hair now, slipping through her fingers where he'd let it grow longer. Fingers digging into his hip. Legs tangling with the scratch of denim of his jeans. Belly pressed to the hardness of his belt buckle, his…

She pulled away suddenly, Jannes's hand still in her hair, his arm still solid against her waist. His cheeks were flushed, his lips red, swollen, bitten, and his eyes still closed as he pulled in a shuddering breath.

CHAPTER TWO

'Now aren't you glad that didn't happen at a family event?' Lara asked, laughing shakily. They could joke about this. They *should* joke about this. It wasn't serious. It wasn't *real*.

He glanced around them. Somehow, life in the park hadn't ceased to exist just because they'd been…swept away. 'This is very public.'

'Safer, I think. Imagine if we'd been…' Alone. She could imagine it. Was imagining it right now in fact. And frightening herself knowing where it could have ended up if they hadn't come to their senses.

It was just the shock, the novelty of it that had made it so explosive, she told herself. And now they had it out of their system, knew what to expect, they'd be better prepared next time. Would guard against getting carried away.

'So.' She uncurled her fingers from his hip, leaned back against the arm clasped at her waist. 'Now we have a first kiss story.'

'Yeah, I suppose we didn't need to get too creative after all.'

'We tell people…friends, feelings for one another, kiss in the park. Here we are.'

'That sounds plausible,' he said, with an expression that it didn't seem safe to interpret just yet. Of course it sounded plausible: if she wasn't so scared of hurting him, of being hurt in return, that was the reality they would be living right now. But she couldn't lose him, so they both pretended that it hadn't meant a thing to either of them. At least, she thought he was pretending.

'Should we walk?' Lara said, taking a deliberate step away from him, needing this friendship back on familiar ground before one of them said something that they couldn't take back. 'I could do with a coffee.'

'Good idea,' Jannes said, avoiding eye contact.

They turned back towards the park, followed a path past squealing toddlers on the playground, a group of teenagers gathered around a speaker, dodged pairs of runners sweating in the late spring warmth. She startled when she felt Jannes's fingers thread through hers and she looked up at him, surprised.

'What's this?' she asked, lifting their linked fingers with trepidation. Was he... did he think that kiss was real? That it had changed something between them? Because she thought that they had been clear. If she wanted to know why he was holding her hand, she could just ask.

'Practice,' he said, and shrugged as they let their hands drop.

'You need to practice holding hands?' she asked, forcing a laugh, trying to make light of this. 'How long *has* it been since you last dated properly, more than a first date?'

She thought back, tried to remember the last time he'd introduced her to a girl. More than a year ago, at least.

'I need to practice holding hands with *you*,' he clarified. 'Need to make it look like we do this all the time. Not like we're—'

'We're walking through the park to get coffee,' she cut in on a nervous laugh, not wanting to hear the end of that sentence. 'We *do* do this all the time.'

Jannes shrugged. 'I don't want to walk in there unprepared.'

'Fine,' she said, sighing. 'You're right. If you want to practice, we can practice. Now, do you need to practice my coffee order? Because I'm hot and this shady bench is looking very tempting. It's still five minutes to the coffee stand.'

'Fine,' Jannes said, and she knew his expressions well enough to recognise relief when she saw it. 'You sunbathe, I'll get the coffee.'

That was…intense.

Jannes stalked off towards the coffee stand, walking faster now that he didn't have to slow for Lara's shorter frame.

He had meant it to be a quick peck on the lips, to prove to himself if no one else that he and Lara were good enough friends to fake being an item without things becoming weird. He hadn't been prepared for the chain reaction that the merest brush of her lips against his had triggered. He hadn't been thinking at all when he'd pinned her body flush against his. When he'd arched into the kiss, wanting to be closer, to lift her higher, to bring every inch of her body into contact with his own. It had taken every gram of strength that he'd had to pull away from her, to remind himself that the reason he'd been resisting her since the day that he'd met her was because he didn't want to hurt her. Because she deserved better than that.

Jesus, it had been a while. Perhaps he could pretend that that was why he had felt so desperate for her. Far from having a girl in every port, the last year he'd been…circumspect. Aware that every date he had would inevitably end up in the tabloids or going viral. A version of his life gaining traction that he just didn't recognise. He hadn't left a string of broken hearts in his wake, regardless of what the papers wrote. It was the opposite, in fact. He'd avoided getting involved past a first date, knowing that he would only hurt someone if he let himself get closer.

The holding hands—where had that come from? He'd given Lara a convenient excuse to cover up the fact that he'd done it without thinking. The kiss had broken through all the defences that he'd constructed, and he'd just acted on instinct. Forgot, for a moment, that he had to resist taking what he wanted. His skin had wanted hers and he'd reached for her before his brain had caught up with what his body was doing.

He reached the stall and ordered their coffees, realising after he'd done it that he hadn't even had to think about what she wanted. He couldn't remember the last time he'd been with a girl long enough to know her coffee order. But this was different. Lara wasn't a girlfriend. She was a friend. A good friend. Probably the best one he'd had, in fact. It was perfectly understandable that he knew what coffee she liked. He spent more time with her than just about anyone else.

And now he had kissed her and his head had exploded and all these years of keeping their relationship carefully platonic had gone up in smoke.

It was friendly, he told himself again. They were kissing and pretending to date because that was what a good friend did when they were asked.

He walked back towards where he had left Lara on the bench and found her stretched out, thumbs tapping at her phone, face screwed up with concentration. He stood and watched her for a moment. She looked focused. No hint that she shared in the roiling anxiety he'd been fighting since their kiss. He was making a big deal out of nothing. To her, it had clearly been what they'd intended: a practice kiss between friends. No feelings involved. She knew the score, and he did too.

CHAPTER THREE

'WOW, YOU LOOK…'

Lara stood by the door of her apartment, eyebrow raised as Jannes looked her up and down, waiting for him to finish his sentence. They really needed to get on their way to the wedding, but there was no way she was leaving until she had heard what Jannes thought.

'…nice,' he finished, and she rolled her eyes.

Nice was the worst of all the compliments. She kind of wished that she'd not let him finish now.

'You too,' she replied with a smirk. 'Shall we go?'

Normally she would have invited him in. Let him lean his long limbs against the kitchen counter while she darted between her bedroom and bathroom, posting pictures of her getting ready, gathering up last-minute bits for her handbag, forgetting her credit card and having to run back for her lipstick.

She was nervous about seeing her family, wanted to get it over and done with. That was what she told herself as she hustled Jannes out of the door. Nothing to do with not trusting herself to be alone in her apartment with him after that kiss. Everything would go back to normal after tonight. They would put this behind them and get back to slobbing around in lounge pants and watching bad TV together at the weekends. Back to maintaining their friendship over video calls while he went from training camp to training camp, around the world solo and back again.

Soon, she'd be able to look at him and find him *nice* again. The way that she had before that kiss. Because, right now, nice didn't seem to be doing him justice, and she wasn't sure what could have changed that other than the kiss that they'd shared.

The suit helped of course. Cut close to his shoulders, the waist and hips slender enough to make her jealous, but which she knew now were hardened muscle underneath. His shirt was pale blue, just enough of a hint of colour to do something to his eyes that made them hard to look away from. That made his skin and his hair glow. Really, sometimes it was very hard being his friend.

She fluffed up her hair and locked the door behind her, checking her lift sharing app to make sure that the driver had found her apartment building. Or to give her eyes somewhere to look that wasn't at Jannes.

'So, anything I need to know before we go in there?' Jannes asked in the car on the way to the ceremony at the groom's parents' manor out in the home counties.

'Oh, you know…the usual: my jackass of a father. Secret second daughter—i.e. me—taken into the bosom of the "official" family when her mum received an eviction notice from the flat that she thought she owned and all was discovered. Step-family determined to make up for his shortcomings by being obsessively kind. Pip, the only child who always dreamed of having a sister, suddenly finding she had one all along and determined to love me.'

Jannes was silent for a second as she collected herself. 'Will he be there?' he asked, his voice so gentle it threatened to spark tears.

'Nope. Haven't seen him for years. He sees

some of the family but I've always managed to dodge him. Pip didn't invite him; she knew I wouldn't come if she did.' And she wouldn't care if she never saw him again. Which was convenient, really, considering that he seemed to feel the same way about her. 'His mother will be. My grandmother, I suppose. Hard to think of her like that though when I spent most of my life being told that she was dead.'

Jannes reached for her hand and squeezed it. She pulled it away before she could do something stupid like turn her palm to his and lace their fingers together. 'I'm sorry today will be hard for you. I think you're really brave for doing this.'

'Brave. Stupid. What's the difference?' She forced a smile to her face, but knew that Jannes wouldn't be fooled.

'You're a good sister, putting yourself through it for Pip. You must really care about her.'

Lara shrugged, shifting her hand out of reach just as he reached for it. 'They took us in. Kicked him out. I owe them.'

Jannes nodded in agreement. Squeezed her hand again.

The car slammed to a halt outside the gates

to Pip's fiancé's family home, stopping her from doing anything stupid. 'You sure you want to do this?' he asked as she reached for the door handle.

She forced a smile. 'Nope, but we're going to anyway.'

'That's my girl.'

CHAPTER FOUR

HIS GIRL.

Well, it was true enough for the next few hours, Jannes supposed, walking through the grounds with Lara's hand in his. He'd half expected that they'd be hidden away in a corner, being unobtrusive, avoiding notice. He wasn't sure why he would think that when three years of friendship with Lara had yet to produce a problem that she didn't think was best tackled head-on with the volume turned up. She marched straight to her grandmother and kissed her dryly on the cheek before introducing him.

'Elaine, this is my boyfriend, Jannes.'

Warm hands clasped his as a kiss was pressed to his cheek.

'I was just saying that it was about time you settled down,' Lara's grandmother said.

'Now you two, come and sit by me and fill me in on your news.'

'Ah—' Jannes said.

At the same time Lara replied, 'We're just going to grab a drink before Pip arrives. But we'll definitely catch up with you later.'

And then he was kissed by a series of aunts and cousins and assorted other strangers before being pushed into a chair near to the front of the assembled rows in the largest marquee and the chatter dropped to a hushed whisper.

'You doing okay?' he asked.

She gave him a tight smile, and then Pip arrived, floating down the aisle in a powderpuff-pink dress. But Jannes's eyes snapped back to Pip's fiancé as he watched her, dumbstruck, grinning dopily. His expression—as if he couldn't believe his luck—didn't change the whole time they were exchanging their vows. It was a good look on him, Jannes decided, slightly envious of the satisfied glow that emanated from the happy couple.

He risked a glance across at Lara, who was watching the proceedings with a fixed smile in place. He linked her fingers with his, trying not to notice how natural that had started to feel. They had done it only a few times since that first time in the park, but it just felt...right. This was why they had been so careful before—because they had both known that the attraction was there, because they both knew that this could be something more if they wanted it to be. And because he knew how much he didn't want that to happen. He didn't want to get closer to Lara, only to be afraid that she would leave him. He didn't want to hurt her, pulling away because of that fear. Being just friends was safer for both of them.

It was easy to see now that they had breached the buffer that had always been between them. How they had always been careful to avoid the accidental touches that sent sparks flying between them. Because now they had crossed that divide and seen—felt—what things were like on the other side, it was hard to remember how it had felt to *not* know. Harder to think about how they were meant to get back to a place where they were ignorant of this. And when he thought about that kiss...

Well, mostly, he just *didn't* think about that kiss, because, well, when he started it was too hard to stop. He'd have a flashback while he was waiting for pasta to cook and find himself half an hour later, staring at a glutinous mass of overcooked starch and wonder how he could lose time thinking about a simple kiss. A kiss that wasn't even supposed to be the real thing. But had nonetheless shaken him to his bones in a way that no other kiss seemed to have ever managed.

Speaking of kisses, the happy couple were now locking lips while somehow simultaneously giggling, and then passing back along the aisle, and he realised he'd missed the last ten minutes and the ceremony was over.

Lara let out a long breath that made him wonder when she'd last inhaled, and he reached an arm around her shoulder in a way that he had meant to be friendly. But he hadn't been counting on the effect of the bare skin of his forearm—he'd rolled his sleeves up in the sweltering garden outside, and Lara had taken her jacket off—against the warm skin of Lara's shoulders. Her jumpsuit had a complicated criss-cross of straps spanning her shoulder blades, revealing golden skin down to the small of her back. Which had never really been a part of the human body that had interested him before, but that he was finding hard to resist. Lara sat stiffly beside him, not leaning into him, and that should have been fine. This whole day was about Lara and if what she needed was this inch of clear space between his ribs and hers, then that was fine. That was what they were doing. It was completely out of order for him to be disappointed that she had passed up the opportunity to lean into him, just because he was curious about how good that might feel.

This wasn't about feeling. It was about appearances. And if an arm around her shoulder was all the situation required then that was all they would do.

Lara gave herself a little shake and turned to him with a slightly more natural smile on her face.

'Bar?' she asked.

'Bar,' Jannes agreed, keeping his arm around her shoulders as they walked towards one of the smaller marquees—just for the sake of authenticity, of course.

'Just so I know,' Jannes asked, as she ordered a beer for him and a bottle of wine for herself, 'is the drinking going to be in any way in moderation? No judgement either way.'

'Absolutely not,' Lara said, pouring herself a large glass and tucking the bottle under her arm as they went to find a seat outside. 'I'm counting on you to make sure I get home later without making too much of a tit of myself.'

'Babysitting duty. Got it.'

She frowned at that. 'Less babysitter. More...wingman.'

'Isn't a wingman meant to help you get laid?' he asked. 'That might undermine our story a little.'

She waved his concern away with a hand. 'You just have to help me find *you*, then. You're my hook-up.'

'I thought I was your boyfriend,' he said, laughing at how quickly Lara had got flushed and silly with the wine.

'Right. Otherwise known as a guaranteed hook-up.'

Jannes rolled his eyes. 'You're so romantic.'

'You're not with me for hearts and flowers. I don't really go in for that.'

'Oh, really?' He regarded her carefully, trying to keep his expression neutral. 'What am I with you for?'

'The wild sex and Instagram freebies.'

He felt his face warm and knew it must be

flushing red. His only hope was that he had caught enough sun this summer that his tan would hide it a little.

'I've embarrassed you!' Lara said with a small squeal of delight and smacked a kiss on his cheek. 'That's adorable.'

'*Don't* call me adorable. You're insufferable.'

'I never said today was going to be easy.'

'You never told me that you were going to be the hardest part.' But he smiled, because even when she was being insufferable he had more fun with her than he knew how to have with anyone else.

'Sorry,' Lara said with a smile and a gulp of wine that suggested she wasn't, in the least.

'Here,' he said, handing her a glass of water, condensation beading the glass.

'Spoilsport,' she said with a frown. 'Some wingman you are.'

'I'm not slowing you down, *sötnos*. But you'll thank me for the hydration in the morning.'

'Fine.' She drank half the glass in one go, and he found himself unreasonably intrigued by the line of her neck as she tipped her head back to drink. 'And don't speak Swedish to me. You know I think you're cute when you do that.'

As she handed back the glass, cheers and applause rippled through the garden and he turned to see Pip and her husband in the doorway, fresh from having their photos taken and ready to party with their guests.

Pip made a beeline for Lara and wrapped her in a tight hug. He saw how Lara stiffened in the presence of her half-sister, and he slid his arm around her waist and squeezed gently, making sure Lara knew he was there for her if she needed him. He leaned in to kiss Pip on the cheek too—they had met a couple of times—and shook hands with the groom.

'Congratulations,' he said, covering for Lara's awkward silence. 'It was a lovely ceremony.'

'It was short,' Pip said with a laugh. 'I'm impatient, and it makes you popular with the guests. And we're not the only ones who need congratulating. It looks like you two have news for us too!' She looked pointedly at where Jannes's arm was still resting on Lara's hip. 'I always said there was something between you two. I'm glad you finally worked it out. We all wondered how long it would take you.'

'All?' Lara said, hiding a laugh. 'You should have said something. Maybe it wouldn't have taken us so long.' Jannes resisted the urge to roll his eyes. Lara couldn't resist the opportunity to tease, even when no one but the two of them were in on the joke.

'We're keeping you from your guests,' Jannes said tactfully as the conversation petered out and a crowd gathered around Pip and her new husband. 'I don't want to be accused of monopolising you.'

'You're right, but I'm going to want to hear all about it later,' Pip said with another hug for her sister. 'You guys look great together,' she said. Adding, 'Look after her. She's special,' with a mock stern look at Jannes before she turned away from the crush of well-wishers.

Jannes looked down at Lara and saw that the hand holding her wine was shaking slightly. Her shoulders were set in a stiff line, and the smile on her face was threatening to slide into a grimace.

'Hey,' Jannes said, turning Lara's face up to his and then wrapping her in a hug. 'You did well. Really well. Pip was so happy to see you here.' He held her tighter still, until he felt the shaking stop. 'Better?' he asked, looking down at the top of her head. Her forehead was pressed against his chest and, before he could think too hard about it, he dropped a kiss to her hair and brought up one hand to cup the nape of her neck.

He wasn't even sure that this was what she had meant, when she'd asked him to pretend to be her boyfriend. That was meant to be for show. To satisfy the curiosity of her family. But holding her like this—this wasn't for show. This was because she needed him, and when it came to Lara he didn't know how to say no to her. And now that the usual boundaries between them had been bulldozed by that kiss, here they were, in the middle of a family wedding, with her head on his chest and his fingers in her hair, learning the texture of it, the feel of it slipping through his fingers as she took a long shuddering breath.

When she looked up the strain had gone from her expression. Instead there was something there he recognised from that day in the park, right before they'd kissed. His hand was still tangled in her hair, hers still rested lightly on his hips. Looking into her eyes, he could see that she was thinking about it too, and when her tongue darted out to moisten parted lips he knew she was tempted. Or she was acting, playing a part. He was here to play a part too, and he leaned down to brush a gentle kiss to her lips.

'Lara!'

She broke away at the sound of her name and Jannes looked up to see Pip's mother and her new partner brandishing a bottle of champagne and a handful of glasses.

'We're so thrilled you're here,' Gloria, Pip's mother, said, kissing Lara on both cheeks and then leaning back to get a good look at her. 'You're looking incredible,' she said, and then glanced up at Jannes. 'And you must be Jannes. I've heard so much about you. Thank you for coming.'

'Thanks for having me,' he said, smiling and shaking hands and silently cursing that they'd been interrupted. And then wanted to kick himself for the selfish thought. He wasn't supposed to care whether or not he was kissing Lara. This was meant to be play-acting.

He reminded himself of that as he made small talk with Lara and her family, his hand resting on the small of her back, as if he wasn't thoroughly distracted by the thought of all that golden skin under the criss-crosses of her jumpsuit.

He was good. Oh, he was really good. She had to remind herself of that. Remind herself not to let herself get dizzy from the warm, lazy circles Jannes was rubbing at the small of her back. He was being supportive. And kind. And he was kissing her and touching her because that was exactly what she'd asked him to do—to pretend to be her boyfriend and to make it convincing… There was nothing personal in the feel of his skin on hers. Even in the way that his lips brushed hers.

Thank God they had talked about this. She didn't have to think about her feelings. About what feelings Jannes might or might not be having. Here, of all places, among these people, she needed that certainty. Having talked with Jannes beforehand about what they were doing, the fake boyfriend was the only solution.

She'd spent her childhood adoring someone who had lied to her every time he had opened his mouth and spoken to her. Every 'I love you' that had come from his lips was worthless. She wasn't going to spend her adulthood repeating those mistakes. And if that meant agreeing in advance that a relationship was a lie, rather than waiting and hoping and then just finding out later, then that was what she would do. What would Jannes think if she told him that? she wondered. If she confessed that she wanted him, but only if they were pretending. Would he settle for that? If that was all that she could give him?

She leaned into Jannes's side, breathing freely again as she watched her stepmother move away, making her way through the assembled guests, kissing cheeks and directing wait staff with trays of champagne and spreading her good mood throughout the crowds.

'You going to finish the bottle now?' Jannes asked, watching her watching Pip's mother and sensing her mood.

'Oh, yeah.'

'Then we should go and find you some carbs.'

He pulled on her hand and she thought he really might be the best man she knew. Which was precisely why she wanted him in her life permanently—which meant as a friend. Where he couldn't break her heart. Couldn't make her love him and then take it away again when she gave in and loved him back. She didn't want to lose him, which meant she was never going to hope for—want—more than she had now.

CHAPTER FIVE

'COME ON THEN, *sötnos*,' Jannes said, one arm around Lara's waist as he helped her from the taxi. 'Let's get you upstairs before you do something disgusting in this nice man's car.'

She laughed, as he knew she would.

'I told you: don't be all Swedish and charming. I'm too drunk not to find it adorable.'

He hoisted Lara against his side as he went through her bag looking for her keys, a job made somewhat more difficult by the fact that Lara kept sinking down, threatening to slip from his grasp every time he thought he had a hand on her keys.

'And I told you hours ago to stop calling me adorable. Here we go,' he said, wrapping her arms around his neck for extra safety as he finally got hold of the keys and opened the door to her apartment.

All in all, the day hadn't been too much of

a disaster. Lara had managed to keep a smile on her face throughout the speeches, including the one that Gloria made in place of Pip and Lara's conspicuously absent father, and as the wine had made her looser and more morose, he had simply wedged her against him in the corner of the dance floor so it would look to anyone who took an interest that they were simply too besotted with one another to be dragged apart rather than the fact that by nine o'clock Lara could no longer stand unassisted. But she'd achieved the status of falling-over-drunk with more panache and style than he'd seen anyone manage before. And he was nothing if not impressed by her stamina.

He staggered through the door with one arm clamped around her waist, and it was more awkward to stoop than it was to simply straighten up and carry her, her toes just brushing the doorjamb as he manoeuvred them into her apartment. He shouldered open the bedroom door and dropped her on the bed, both of them letting out an undignified 'Oof!' as he dropped her. Good job no one was trying to impress anyone. If this had been a normal date...

He batted away her hands as she tried to

unbuckle her sandals and pulled them off for her and then averted his eyes and escaped to the kitchen while Lara wrestled out of her jumpsuit. By the time he returned with a pint of water and a couple of paracetamols, Lara was in bed with her hair pulled into a messy bun and the lace-trimmed strap of a tank top slipping from her shoulder. He pulled the strap back into place and the duvet up higher, before handing her the pills and the water.

'You are the best boyfriend I've ever had,' she said as she took the pills from him, and he laughed. But she shoved his arm. 'Don't laugh. It's true. I owe you. You really took care of me tonight. You are an excellent friend and I love you.'

He bit down on his lip to stop himself laughing again—Lara was clearly not in the mood to find her drunken rambling amusing. He kissed her on the forehead with a murmured, 'Goodnight,' and grabbed a blanket from the bottom of the bed. With the amount of wine she'd put away tonight, she was going to be in no state to make the cup of coffee he knew she'd be gasping for the minute she woke up tomorrow, and he had no intention of losing that boyfriend of the year award he'd only just won.

He walked back through to the living room to the sound of Lara snoring and glanced at the notifications on his phone that he'd been ignoring all day. There was one from his manager, asking how many tickets he wanted for the awards show next week. He replied that he'd need a plus one, and could his manager sort out accommodation for them? If tonight had been a test of concept, he was pretty sure they'd passed, and one more fake date couldn't do any harm.

Today had been fun. It wasn't exactly hard to pretend to enjoy hanging out with his best friend. All they had to do was keep this up a little longer and he would be the reformed bad boy. Tamed by the sweetheart of the social media influencer world.

He lay back on the sofa cushions, pulling the throw blanket from Lara's bed over himself and falling, satisfied, into sleep.

She was dying. It was the only possible explanation for this experience in her mouth. It went beyond taste. It was…stale and…furry and…if she didn't think about something else right now she was going to throw up.

She looked round at the sound of a tap on the door and scrunched up her eyes at the sight of Jannes in the doorway. How did he look so fresh this early in the day? Bastard.

'Good morning, sunshine,' he said with a smirk that totally deserved the pillow that she launched at his head. 'Careful, that's your coffee you're spilling.'

'Oh, my God.' She scrambled upright, arms hooked around bent knees. 'Gimme. Please?' she added when all he did was raise an eyebrow at her.

'So, yesterday went well,' Jannes said, sitting on the edge of her bed and putting the coffees down on the bedside table.

'You'd have to tell me. Did I disgrace myself?'

'You were wonderful. You always are. Everybody loved you.'

'You're being very nice,' she said suspiciously, sniffing at her coffee and trying to decide whether her stomach could handle it yet.

'Yes, well, I'm still hoping for that second

date. I told my manager I'm bringing a plus one to the awards. Is that still okay?'

'I don't know. Probably?' she said, leaning back on her pillows. 'Am I still drunk?'

'Possibly. You were far enough gone last night to agree to go to at least one more wedding and a christening this summer. I'm making you another coffee and a bacon sandwich. Then you're having a shower.'

'Ugh, why did I do that? Why did you let me do that? And is that a hint?' she asked, trying to discreetly sniff herself.

'Nope, it's an order. You smell bad. And you agreed to those other events because you are a very good person.'

She collapsed back on the pillows, arm across her face. 'I take it back. You're the worst boyfriend ever.'

She let the water run over her head into her eyes, and by the time she was squeezing her hair dry with a towel she felt almost human again. Jannes was in the kitchen when she emerged, dressed in comfy cashmere pants and a sweater. She could smell bacon and coffee, and the toaster popped as she walked past it, making her jump.

'Tell me more about this awards thing,' she said, taking the coffee he held out to her.

'I'm presenting one of the awards,' Jannes said. 'All you need to do is show up, hold my hand. If anyone asks maybe tell them I'm the best boyfriend you've ever—'

'Worst boyfriend.'

'Best boyfriend you've ever had. I'm getting it embroidered on a pillow. Just stand with me for a few photos, look madly in love with me. Post them on your social media feeds so people get the general idea of how wonderful and dependable and not flaky I am.'

'And that's it,' she clarified. 'Just the awards ceremony and then we're done?'

'If you want it to be,' Jannes said, but a couple of fine lines appeared between his eyebrows. His thinking face. 'Or, if it goes well,' he went on, 'perhaps we carry on playing rent-a-date for each other. Like, at the other family events you agreed to yesterday? I can come to those, if you'd like, when I'm home. And you can come to work things with me. We have fun—you know I love hanging out with you. And, not to be too mercenary about it, but the longer this goes on, the better I look.'

It was her turn to frown, and she rubbed at her forehead, where the throbbing headache she'd woken up with was starting to ease. 'What happens when we don't want people to think we're together any more?'

'Then we gracefully part ways and decide that we were better off as friends. Behind closed doors, nothing has changed.'

Lara nodded, finishing one cup of coffee and pouring herself another. 'And are you sure…' How should she put this? '… I'm not going to be stepping on anyone's toes if we do this? I don't want to find myself as the other woman,' Lara said.

Jannes crossed his arms. 'Are you asking me if I'm seeing someone?'

'Seeing anyone, sleeping with anyone.' Lara waved a vague hand. 'Sending suggestive messages on dating apps to anyone. I mean, you can do what you want, but even if we're just pretending, I don't want it to ever look like we're cheating. At—'

'I'm not seeing anyone,' Jannes said, his expression hard. 'And I won't, as long as we're keeping this up. I wouldn't have agreed to yesterday if I was.'

She took a deep breath and passed him a knife as he reached for the butter. 'Okay. I knew that. I think I knew that. I just had to be sure.'

'It's fine.' He didn't look as if it was fine. And right here was the reason that she didn't date for real. Because she'd had to ask that question, even though she knew that she could trust Jannes. Even though she *knew* he'd never be any less than honest, she'd still had to ask the question. Because she'd *known* that she could trust her father too, and look where that had got them. She'd put that hurt look on Jannes's face, and she had no interest in doing it again. 'I understand why you had to ask,' he said, which didn't change the fact that he was hurt that she couldn't just trust him.

The ease that had been there between them when she'd woken up, when he really had been boyfriend of the year, and she'd been happy to let him, had disappeared. She'd pierced it with this reminder that she would never be able to trust, and that eventually that scar in her soul always ended up with her pushing away anyone who got too close. The closer she let Jannes get, the more she was going to hurt him eventually. She had to remember that.

'So what happens when you meet someone?' she asked, moving the focus of the conversation away from herself, making sure that their terms for this relationship were crystal clear. If they had everything on the table from the start, there was no way that this could become something that it shouldn't.

'What, before Saturday?' Jannes crossed his arms as he looked at her, and she could see him trying to understand the change in the atmosphere. '*If* I meet someone, or you do, we'll talk to each other and work something out. I won't hurt you, Lara. I won't ever hurt you.'

She nodded, took another sip of coffee. 'I know you won't. So how does this work? You'll pick me up?'

'It's in Liverpool. I have to be there early to go through the presenting stuff. I don't want you to have to sit around getting bored. I'll get them to arrange a car for you. Meet you there. Does that work for you?'

'Fine. Fine. I guess I'll see you there.'

CHAPTER SIX

IF THE BACK of Lara's wedding jumpsuit had been sent to test him, then surely this dress was going to end him. He was talking to his manager when she arrived. From the corner of his eye he had spotted long tanned legs, and it was only when his eyes had reached her face that he realised he was looking at Lara. He stopped talking abruptly, and when he heard his manager call his name for the third time he realised he'd been staring.

At the top, the dress was positively demure, cut high on the neck with sleeves past her wrist bones. Midnight-blue crystals covered her body, down over her hips to the top of her thighs, where the dress stopped abruptly, revealing those long soft thighs and the same strappy sandals he'd slipped from her ankles last Saturday night. She waved when she spotted him, and he forced his legs to move.

'Hey, you're here,' he said, leaning in to kiss her on the cheek, remembering at the last minute that she was meant to be his date. He kissed her on the lips, but pulled away before he could be tempted to turn it into anything more than the lightest peck, a mere brush of skin against hers, gone practically before it had started.

'You look beautiful,' he said, eyes fixed on her face now. Her eyes were wide, lined with smoky black and grey, with long, long lashes that fluttered when she blinked.

'You don't look too bad yourself,' she said, leaning back and tweaking the lapel of his dinner jacket. 'I always loved you in black tie.' He was just at the point where he was going to have to start untangling which parts of this were real and which were for show when his manager clapped him on the shoulder and held his hand out to shake with Lara.

'You must be Lara. Glad the car got you here okay.' He looked from Lara to Jannes with a smile on his face. 'Okay, I'm going to let you guys catch up. Jannes can show you to your table. Look forward to talking to you more later, Lara.'

Jannes looked her up and down again, trying to form just one coherent thought and turn it into words.

'You look amazing,' he said.

She laughed awkwardly. 'We did that bit already. What else have you got?'

'Um, let's find you a drink?'

'Ah, much better,' Lara said with a laugh. 'But let's make mine a sparkling water. If I'm the wingman tonight, I'm going to need to stay sober.'

'Of course, the squeaky-clean image I'm meant to be cultivating,' Jannes said. 'But you don't have to do or not do anything on my behalf. You're perfect as you are,' he said. 'Just be yourself.'

'Ah, there you go with the boyfriend of the year script again.' But her cheeks had pinkened. Yes. Right. Because they were faking this. He loved her—as a friend. His hormones were briefly confused by the fact that they had kissed. But they weren't doing any more than playing a part here—if he forgot that, Lara would end up getting hurt, and he wasn't prepared to risk that. 'You get the credit for briefing me in advance.' He guided her towards the bar with a hand on the small of her back.

'Well, if we're going to make it look realistic...'

Because this wasn't real, and he could never forget that he had good reasons for that. He had learned the hard way what happened when you cared more about someone than they cared back. He'd learned it when his parents had shipped him off to boarding school so that they could continue the travelling that they had put on hold when he had been born seven years earlier. He had spent his holidays with his *mormor*, his grandmother, in London. And saw his parents whenever their travel schedule allowed, which was something like twice a year by the time he was in his teens.

Which was why he could be sure that he could commit to this fakery with Lara. Even if he met someone who made him wonder if things could be different, he had long since given up acting on those feelings. What was the point when he already knew how it would end? So why hadn't he just said that to Lara? Because it just seemed sad, somehow, to admit that at the age of thirty he was so afraid of being left—or of hurting someone to stop that happening—that he never even

started a relationship. This thing with Lara
was nothing like that.

She couldn't leave him if it wasn't real, if
they were only acting. He couldn't hurt her
when they both knew that they were going to
stop pretending just as soon as their arrangement was no longer convenient. He had to
make sure he remembered that.

He showed Lara to their table as the ballroom started to fill with people, and he introduced her to his manager, agent and
teammates. She saw the sidelong glances
being thrown their way and wondered what
they made of the situation. There was something about the knowing looks on his col-
leagues' faces that made her wonder if she
was missing something.

The room hushed as the lights dimmed and
the awards ceremony began.

Lara was hyperconscious, now that she was
sitting next to Jannes, of just how much skin
her dress left exposed. Because every time
Jannes leaned in to whisper something about
one of the nominees or winners, the soft fab-
ric of his trousers brushed against her bare
thigh and made her shiver in response. It was

just an involuntary physical reaction, she told herself. A reflex. Practically a sneeze. It shouldn't make her think about his hands touching her there. She had to stop letting her brain do this to her. She was meant to be in charge here. And yet her body and her brain kept ganging up on her and trying to make her believe that indulging these fantasies about Jannes were a good idea. And if both her brain and her body were working against her, she didn't know which part of her was meant to fight these urges.

He was her friend. That was what made this whole 'date for a date' thing a good idea. Neither of them had unrealistic expectations of the other. Neither of them had to air their commitment issues, because it wasn't real. It was company and it was convenient and it didn't need any more consideration than that.

Jannes went and did his presentation thing: she clapped him enthusiastically as he took to the stage and received his kiss on the cheek when he returned with hardly a flutter where she shouldn't be fluttering.

In fact, she was just congratulating herself for how very responsible she was being when she realised she'd spaced out for a minute and missed something. Because on the big screen behind the stage was a picture of Jannes, soaking wet in a white dress shirt, and she couldn't be sure that she wasn't drooling a little. She snapped her mouth shut and smudged the corner of her lips with her finger, hoping it would look as if she was just fixing her lipstick.

She glanced across at Jannes and found him staring at her and thought that maybe she hadn't got away with it after all. She looked back at the screen and kind of wished she hadn't, because now Jannes was shirtless, still dripping wet, and more ripped than his narrow frame suggested. It didn't exactly hurt that he was hanging off the side of a racing yacht, in a photoshoot that made it look as if he was in the process of winning one of those trophies that took up an entire wall of his house.

She worked out what was going on before Jannes did, which was perfect, because it meant that she got to watch as realisation dawned and just the very tips of his ears went red as he was announced as the winner of the special achievement award. The assembled guests burst into applause and whoops of celebration as she pushed Jannes to his feet. She stood too, and gave him a little push towards the stage. He leaned forward and pressed a kiss to her lips and she didn't know whether it was because he was dazed or doing it for show or…she didn't know why else. He was just maintaining their story, keeping their pretence going. It wasn't real. It didn't mean anything. She had to remember that, because at this minute her feelings were all too real.

Jannes took to the stage to accept his award, and his eyes still had that wide, startled quality as he stepped up to the microphone. He thanked his manager and his agent, the award organisers. And then, after a split-second hesitation: 'And Lara, for everything she is to me.'

She stood staring at him, her face frozen in surprise. When he kissed her on the cheek and laced his fingers through hers as he came back to the table, her thoughts were too much in disarray to come up with a coherent question. Until she remembered that this was all for show. He was just sticking to their story, proving once again that he really was the best friend a woman could wish for—far too good to risk losing over something as superficial as how he looked in a wet shirt. She fixed a smile on her face and sat back beside Jannes, her hand still in his, aware of the photographer just to one side.

This was fine. This was simple. This was the reason she'd taken a fake date to Pip's wedding: because she was choosing a life where she didn't have to guess and second-guess people's feelings. Where she didn't have to worry about the fact that second-guessing people's feelings usually led to them getting hurt. She already knew that Jannes was faking his feelings for her, exactly as they had agreed. Which really should have made her feel better. Grounded. But somehow, just... didn't. She shook herself. It turned out that fake relationships were sometimes confusing, complicated, too. But still, compared to the real thing—she thought about the way her father had treated her, and her mother, and Pip's mother, and decided that a fake relationship was the lesser of two evils.

She stuck to Jannes's side as the party wound down, as he accepted congratulations and handshakes and slaps on the back from all directions. Lara felt a swell of pride seeing everything that Jannes had achieved. There was no denying that he deserved the award he'd been presented with that night.

He turned to her finally, when he'd shaken almost every hand in the room.

'Mr Henriksson, I can show you to your room if you're ready,' the hotel manager said, coming over to shake Jannes's hand. Lara wondered if he was glancing at his phone to ward off the awkwardness that had suddenly popped up between them at the mention of the hotel rooms arranged by the awards organisers. 'Congratulations on your award,' the hotel manager went on, beaming at them. 'We've upgraded you to our best suite.'

Lara was on the verge of asking about her own room when she remembered about their pretence. The whole point of her being there was to convince everyone that they were a couple. Separate rooms was going to undo all their hard work, so she squeezed Jannes's hand and followed the hotel manager to the lifts.

When they closed the door of their suite behind them, she looked up at Jannes and burst out laughing. What else could she do? This had started with her agreeing to pretend to be Jannes's girlfriend for a few hours and had so far escalated to a family wedding, a ballroom and now the honeymoon suite of a luxury hotel.

'Wow. This is…' Jannes started, before his voice trailed off. Lara glanced up at him and smiled at the pink flush of his freckled cheeks.

'Extravagant?' Lara suggested.

'That's one word for it,' Jannes said in a low voice that suggested there were several other words that he could think of.

She burst out laughing, because it was the only thing she could think of to break the tension.

'So,' Lara went on, when her laughter eventually petered out. 'Um…what do we do here?'

Jannes looked around him at the extravagant suite with its four-poster bed and free-standing copper bathtub. Lashings of rose petals and crystal and polished wood. 'Lara, I'm so sorry,' he said. 'It never occurred to me to say something about the sleeping arrangements—I should have checked.'

'Relax, Jannes. It's just one night,' Lara said, turning on the spot to take in the whole of the room. 'We don't need to turn this into a big deal.'

'You're right. I'll just sleep on the sofa,' Jannes offered.

She laughed. 'You're at least a foot longer than the sofa,' she pointed out. 'And it's velvet. You'll slip right off in your sleep. There's really no need. I'm sure I can be trusted to spend tonight in a king-size bed with you without trying to jump your bones.'

He laughed at that, but she could still hear the tension in his voice. No wonder, because jumping his bones was exactly what she wanted to do right now, and her and Jannes were good enough friends that she wouldn't be at all surprised if he knew it.

'It's not you I'm worried about,' she could have sworn she heard him murmur. No way was she calling him out on that—that would be *way* too dangerous. Better altogether just to ignore it.

'Come on, Jannes. We're friends. Let's not make a big deal out of this. It's not like there's any danger of something happening between us.'

Well, not now there wasn't. When she made it so clear that she wasn't interested. There had been times that evening when having Lara

by his side had felt so right, so uncompli-
cated, that it made him start to question all
the reasons why he was so sure that seeing if
there might be something more than friendship there between them was a good idea. But
there was no point letting his thoughts wander
in that direction. Even if Lara did see him as
more than a friend, he wasn't going to risk her
walking away from him by suggesting that
having her in his life as a friend didn't always
feel quite…enough. And he wasn't going to
risk losing her by letting them get closer, and
then pushing her away. He couldn't lose her—
it wasn't worth the risk.

'So,' he said, hand rubbing at the back of
his neck. 'What do you want to do for the
rest of the night? Are you tired? I'm still a
bit wired from all…that.'

A knock at the door interrupted the awkward moment, and a hotel employee came in,
pushing a cart with a bucket of champagne
and two tall crystal glasses.

Lara thanked him and took out the card
propped up against the ice bucket. Well, there
were worse things than room service and a
movie and free champagne.

'Telly in bed?' she suggested. 'And open this?'

'Absolutely,' Jannes said, holding up the glasses while she popped the cork.

She poured the champagne and then took a full glass, lifting it towards Jannes in a toast. 'To...us?' she suggested, hoping that Jannes could hear the heavy irony in her voice.

'To us,' he agreed with a smile, clinking their glasses together.

What did she want to do with Jannes in the honeymoon suite of a luxury hotel? Well, wasn't that the question. What she wanted to do and what was actually a good idea were at opposite ends of the spectrum. On the one hand, she had an evening's worth of inappropriate fantasies involving Jannes, a white shirt and a shower. On the other hand, acting out even one of those fantasies would turn this situation from complicated to...impossible. So that pretty much left them with the minibar and a movie.

She stalled in the bathroom, taking her time brushing her teeth and pulling on the shorts and crop top pyjamas she had packed when she'd thought that she'd have a bed to herself.

Jannes slipped past her as she walked back into the bedroom and she was left watching his retreating back.

She climbed onto the bed, pulling a blanket around her shoulders and nudging the throw cushions in between the two firm duck-feather pillows.

'I can still sleep on the floor, you know,' Jannes said, leaning in the doorway of the bathroom, wearing just a T-shirt and boxers.

This wasn't a good idea at all. But saying so would only suggest to him that there was something other than friendship between them that made this a big deal.

'You're making a big deal out of nothing,' Lara told him, desperately trying to convince herself at the same time. She wasn't going to act on temptation—if she did she would end up hurting him, and that just wasn't acceptable. So instead she found the remote for the TV and grabbed some snacks from the minibar. If they were stuck in this awkward situation she was going to make the best of it. And champagne and snacks in bed definitely counted as the best of it.

She scrolled through the TV guide, looking for a movie, before stumbling on an episode of the dating show she was guiltily addicted to. She popped the lid to her Pringles and took a sip of champagne as the opening credits rolled.

'Budge up,' Jannes said, reaching for a handful of crisps. 'Hey, you're two episodes ahead of me. What did I miss?'

She froze with her crisp halfway to her mouth, her jaw hanging open.

'Seriously? You watch this? How did I not know that?'

'Don't judge,' he said with a little huff. 'You watch it too.'

'Yes, but you're—'

He raised an eyebrow. 'Careful there, do I hear some incoming sexism? *What* am I, exactly?'

'You're a relationship-phobe,' she said. 'And yet you want to watch members of the public falling in love?'

He snorted. 'They're hardly in love, most of them. And anyway, pot, kettle et cetera.' He waved a hand, which she assumed stood in for all her commitment issues. Well, those commitment issues were the only thing standing between him and getting hurt, so he probably should be a little kinder about them.

'We're not talking about me,' she reminded him. 'Oh, my God, this guy's my favourite,' she said, taking another sip of her champagne, hoping that it would dissolve the atmosphere that seemed to have suddenly thickened around them.

'You can't like him. He's an idiot. I forbid it.'

'Excuse me?' She widened her eyes, wondering if she was seeing him for the first time. 'You forbid it?'

'I'm your boyfriend now,' he said with a shrug, his eyes never leaving the TV. 'That means I can forbid things. At the very least I can forbid you from talking about other guys that you fancy when we're in bed together.'

She shoved him with her shoulder. 'No wonder you're single, thinking that you get to go around forbidding things. The women of the yachting world have had a lucky escape. Anyway, we're not in bed. We're on the bed.'

'Oh, yes, of course. That's a very important distinction.'

She rolled her eyes. '*In* bed and *on* bed are worlds apart. Everybody knows that.'

'Well, I don't know that. I'm not an expert,

but I am fairly sure you're not meant to talk to me about other guys.'

'Jealous?' she asked, wondering why she felt a twist of nervous anticipation in her belly as she waited for his answer.

'Not at all,' Jannes said at last, leaning back on the pillow with his eyes safely back on the screen. 'I don't need to be. I know he's not your type.'

She laughed and elbowed him in the ribs. 'Oh, really? And what's my type?'

'You know. Tall, blond, sporty. Swedish, preferably.' The corners of his lips turned up infinitesimally, so no one but her would have been able to tell that he was joking.

She jabbed him with her elbow. 'Ugh. Stop talking, I can't hear the TV.' But he swiped her back with a cushion, catching her just as she was taking a sip of champagne and spilling the whole lot down her pyjama top.

'Argh,' she cried, kneeling up and brushing off the front of her crop top. 'I'm soaked! You did that on purpose!'

'I didn't—I'm sorry!'

She dived into the bathroom——leaving Jannes looking crestfallen on the bed——and rinsed out her top, before hanging it in the shower to drip dry. It was only once the emergency was dealt with that she realised she was wearing not much more than a slightly damp bralette underneath. And now she was in her underwear, in a hotel room with Jannes, and had no idea where she was going to find something dry to wear.

Jannes appeared at the bathroom door, his eyes fixed firmly on the floor. 'Everything okay?' he asked. 'Could it be rescued?'

'No harm done,' she said, crossing her arms over her chest, and then spotting the towelling robes on the back of the door. Jannes's eyes grew wide as she came towards him, and then a look of relief washed over his features as she grabbed the robe and tied it firmly around her waist.

'Do you want me to get you something from your case?' he asked her, his ears slightly pink, giving him away.

'I didn't bring a spare,' she said. 'Wasn't anticipating pyjama disasters.' But they would have to do something, because it was hard enough ignoring these feelings for Jannes that were only growing stronger. Spending the night with him in only her underwear would be unbearable.

'Want to borrow a T-shirt?' Jannes asked, and she could have kissed him with gratitude, if that wouldn't have made things infinitely more complicated. She took half a second to think about how intimate it was, borrowing his clothes to sleep in. But if the alternative was this flimsy underwear, she didn't really have much of a choice.

'Thanks, yeah, that'd be great.'

CHAPTER SEVEN

LARA WOKE TO the smell of oranges—the smell of Jannes, his shower gel or his laundry powder, she'd never been able to work out exactly what—and a complete lack of feeling in her left arm. She opened her eyes a crack before squeezing them back shut. She couldn't be responsible for what she did when she was sleeping, she told herself. Except she might have been dreaming about Jannes— things were a little hazy—so that did make her kind of culpable if she'd somehow started acting out her fantasies. But that wasn't important now.

What was important was extracting herself from this situation without waking him. She took an inventory of body parts. Her left arm was trapped under his chest, hence the lack of feeling. Her right had fallen into the notch of his waist. Her left leg was tucked in behind his knees, but her right was clamped between hard thighs. She tried an experimental pull, but Jannes's legs tightened around hers and he pulled her closer with the arm trapped beneath his body. He smelled of oranges, and the soft hair at the nape of his neck was tickling her face.

She had to get herself out of this before Jannes woke up. The last thing that this situation needed was for there to be two of them conscious of how unbelievably close and unbelievably hot this was. Because while this was one-sided it was something that she could undo. If they were both awake, both aware of how close they were to…to something stupid, then she wasn't sure if her self-control would hold and she wouldn't do something to embarrass herself—something that could break her heart and their friendship.

She took just half a moment to imagine a world where things were different. Where something deep inside herself hadn't broken when her father had left her. Where Jannes wasn't scarred by being left again and again by his parents. Where they were both whole and healthy and ready to trust. If she had been that person, if he had been that man, she knew that they would be happy. She knew that there was no one on the planet who was more perfect for her than Jannes was. But they weren't those people. And trying to make this friendship any more than it already was would result in both of them getting hurt. And losing Jannes from her life... Removing herself from the bed was the only safe course of action.

She withdrew the arm that was resting on top of Jannes's waist and laid it against his back, using it to gently push him away. If she could just free her leg, she could snatch her arm from underneath him and it wouldn't matter if that woke him because she had every intention of being out of the room before he even realised what was going on. But she couldn't take that approach with both arm and leg: too high risk. Too much of a chance of getting caught.

She tried easing away from him again, this time pushing gently at his shoulder as she tried to move her leg. But he just held on to her tighter, wrapping her trapped arm around his middle and scooting back closer to her. So he was a touchy-feely sleeper. She tried really hard not to file that fact away for future ref-

erence. She let her forehead rest against the
nape of his neck as she took stock of her fail-
ure and reconsidered her tactics. When she
moved away, he pulled her closer. So if she
wanted to get out, she would have to get…
closer? Oh, this was going to end in tears, she
was sure of it.

She rested her arm back on his waist and
tightened it experimentally. Jannes took a
deep breath in and let it out as a long sigh.
Interesting. She pressed her chest harder
against his back, keeping her forehead close
to the soft hair at the nape of his neck. She
was never going to be able to eat an orange
again after this. But the longer she held him,
the more his grip on her relaxed. She just had
to stick this out.

The next time he breathed out, she pressed
herself against him again, trying hard not to
notice the shift of his muscles under his shirt,
the tensing of his abs as she pressed her hand
against them. But the vice around her trapped
thigh loosened, and slowly, slowly, she drew
her leg back.

Jannes shifted restlessly when she finally
got it free, and she tucked her cheek into the
notch where his neck met his shoulder until

his stirring stopped. This was torture. It was everything that she wanted, but knew that she couldn't have. If she had to design a torture for herself this would be it. Being so close to Jannes that she was practically inhaling him without being able to do anything—to keep them from both getting hurt. Worse—having to rely on her own slightly shaky self-control to keep them both in line.

She listened and waited as Jannes's breathing slowed and deepened. The soft hairs on his thigh tickled her sensitive skin and she bit her lip to stop herself sighing. She had to keep her eye on the prize here. And the prize was unquestionably extracting herself from this situation without doing something that couldn't be taken back. Without doing something that would lose her Jannes for ever.

But it was so tempting not to fight this. Just go back to sleep with her body smooshed up against Jannes's. To wait for them both to wake up like this and…allow the inevitable to happen.

But then what if she started to feel…*more* for Jannes? And he'd inevitably start to pull away—she'd seen him with girls before; she knew his MO too well to question what would happen. And she would be left, leaving her hurt and confused—and without her best friend there to help put her back together. She was smarter than that. Too smart to keep doing the same thing over and over and expecting different results.

She took a final deep breath, pulled her leg back and breathed a long sigh of relief. She'd done it, and Jannes hadn't even twitched. She was so close to being free from him.

Except she wasn't, was she? Because even when she was out of his bed she was still in his life. She'd agreed to date him. To bring him to family parties, to show up on red carpets and photo calls with him. She could do that as a friend. As long as they were doing it in separate beds from now on.

She pulled her arm out from underneath him and rolled towards the edge of the bed, her eyes on Jannes to see if he would wake. Nothing. Not even a twitch. She let out her held breath in a rush and darted from the bedroom, knowing how dangerous it would be to stay.

Jannes woke to unfamiliar surroundings, unable to shake the feeling that he had lost something important. It was only as he clicked where he was—the honeymoon suite of the Liverpool hotel—that he realised what was missing: Lara. He sat up in bed, looking round until he heard movement in the next room and realised she must be up already. No wonder he'd slept in later than her. He'd been awake half the night, listening to her breathing beside him, fighting the urge to deconstruct their pillow barrier and pull her close.

She had fallen asleep while they were still bickering good-naturedly about the relative merits of the slime-balls on the dating show that they'd both admitted to liking. And then she'd snored on, oblivious to the fact that they were in bed together.

Had she felt awkward when she'd woken up this morning? Was that why she was in the next room instead of lounging in bed, taking advantage of the opportunity for a lazy Sunday morning? He swung himself out of bed and pulled on jeans from his bag. Lara was in the sitting room of their suite, coffee in hand as she listened to the radio, head tipped back against the sofa, eyes closed.

'You're still tired,' he said, leaning against the doorway and watching her. Her eyes snapped open and he thought for a second that she was going to spill her coffee, but somehow she managed to rescue it. 'Sorry, I didn't mean to startle you. Was I hogging the duvet?'

They could make light of this. They could pretend that they could share a bed without it meaning anything, as if they were the simply platonic friends that they had always told each other they were. He didn't know why he had brought up the subject of their sleeping arrangements at all when it was clearly so much simpler if they both pretended that they had never shared a bed, but it just felt like…something that needed acknowledging. It was too big to ignore.

She let her eyes drift back closed. 'It's fine. Just a late night. Wasn't expecting the raucous after-party.'

He laughed and crossed the room, prising her coffee cup from her hand. 'I'm just getting you a refill,' he said at her squawked protest. 'You should go back to bed for a bit,' he added, placing the coffee on the table beside her. 'Now that I'm up.'

'It's okay, I'm awake now. Won't be able to get back to sleep.'

He laughed again. 'Right. You look very awake.'

She opened one eye. 'Don't start. So what have you—?' she started to ask, when his phone started ringing.

He glanced at the screen. 'It's Mormor,' he said. 'I should get this.'

'Tell her I say hi,' Lara said with a smile of genuine affection, eyes drifting back closed.

'*Hej*, Mormor,' he said, answering the phone.

Lara listened to the sing-song of Jannes speaking Swedish. She'd picked up a few phrases over the course of her friendship with him, but nowhere near enough to follow when he was speaking rapid-fire to his grandmother. He was agitated, she realised. His smile was fixed in place and his tone was still cheerful. But somehow unnaturally so. She wished she knew what he was saying. And, for that matter, why she kept hearing her own name every time his eyes slid over to her.

He hung up the phone and then pinched the bridge of his nose, looking like a teenager who knew he was about to get into trouble with his parents. Or his stern Swedish grand-mother.

'Jannes? What have you done?' she asked, not sure whether she was more amused or worried by the expression on his face.

'That was Mormor,' he said, his expression bleak.

'I know. What's wrong?'

'She saw us—pictures from last night.'

Lara shrugged. 'So what? I mean, I didn't think she would have seen them already, but pictures of us was kind of the point, right?'

'Apparently she follows you on Instagram. I thought I'd have a chance to talk to her before she found out.'

Lara nodded, still not quite seeing what the problem was. 'And *this*—' she gestured at him, his bleak expression and anxious posture '—is because she thinks we're together?'

He shook his head.

'Jannes, just tell me or I'm going to start panicking.'

'She summoned us for lunch,' he said in an ominous tone. 'Today.'

'Today? I was going to—I need to study.'

What she actually wanted to say was that she needed space. Distance. To catch her breath and try not to think about waking up stuck to Jannes like a barnacle. An impromptu lunch with his grandmother didn't exactly fit in to that plan.

'I tried to argue,' Jannes said, 'but she was…quite persistent. Apparently that's not the way she should find out that…'

'What?'

He frowned. 'It's hard to translate.'

'Try,' Lara said through gritted teeth, and Jannes shook his head, giving in.

'To find out that I've stopped being an idiot and…'

'And?'

'And finally seen what was staring me in the face all this time.'

Lara stared, not sure what to say. 'Jannes…'

'I know.'

She softened towards him, knowing how much his grandmother meant to him. 'You don't have to lie to your family just because I'm lying to mine. It's not as if Mormor is going to go to the papers. You can just tell her the truth.'

'I know. I know that. And I tried to explain that it's not what it seems but… I don't know what happened…she somehow just refused to hear it.'

'Well, you can explain properly when you go to lunch.'

'*We're* going to lunch.'

Lara frowned at him. 'She's not *my* grandmother. She can't make me.'

'I'm sorry, are we back in the playground?' Jannes asked, clearly frustrated. 'Of course she can't make you. But she isn't going to believe me if I go on my own. She'll convince herself that I'm over-complicating things and I should settle down and produce offspring immediately. Trust me, she already laid the groundwork on the phone. If we're both there she can't insist that we're both wrong about whether we're together or not.'

She shook her head. How had she ever expected dating Jannes—even fake dating him—to be simple? 'You know this is ridiculous, don't you?' she said. 'I have other friends, Jannes, quite a few of them, and I've never had to go for Sunday lunch to convince any of their grandmothers that I'm not sleeping with them.'

He smiled, and somehow that felt like a

victory. 'It's not my fault you've led such a sheltered life, is it?' he said.

She threw a cushion at him. 'God. Fine. I'll come. But only because your grandmother is absurd. I cannot believe I'm agreeing to this.'

He walked over, all fluid and graceful and disgustingly composed, and placed the cushion back beside her. 'You're the best,' he said, nudging her feet so she'd make room for him on the sofa. 'I told her we'd be leaving in an hour and would get a car straight to hers.'

She sat abruptly upright. 'Jesus, Jannes. An hour? Straight to hers? I've got to go home and change.'

'No, you don't.'

'I'm wearing your T-shirt. I *slept* in this T-shirt. It's hardly going to convince her that we're just good friends.'

He settled further into the corner of the sofa and took her coffee off her, stealing a sip before placing it on the end table. 'Well, you must have brought other clothes.'

'I brought *getting a cab back home* clothes. Not *going for lunch with your eccentric grandmother* clothes. Jannes, I can't—'

'Stop. You're perfect.'

He cut her off and she stared at him for

a moment, not quite sure where her next thought was supposed to come from when her brain had just turned to mush in the space between one word and the next.

'I mean—I just meant—you'll be fine. Whatever you wear.'

'Fine?'

'Yeah.'

Cool, so they were just going to not talk about the perfect thing. That was a good idea. It was just a slip of the tongue. Or something you just say to a mate. They were on their way to go convince his *mormor*—the person he was closest to in the world—that they weren't really together. If she ever needed an ego check, well, there was one ready-made.

CHAPTER EIGHT

'I CAN'T BELIEVE I'm doing this in ratty old jeans,' Lara said as they climbed the stairs towards Mormor's apartment. She lived across two floors of an old town house in west London, with a view of the gated garden to the front through the big Georgian windows, and out to a little mews at the back, with Farrow & Ball painted doors and bay trees in tubs outside each house.

'Should I point out that I'm also wearing jeans?' Jannes asked. 'Or will that get me in trouble?'

Lara rolled her eyes. 'She dotes on you—you can wear what you like. I'm meant to be making a good impression.'

Or at least that was what it felt like. The whole thing had a decidedly *meet the parents* feel to it. Which was ridiculous, truly, because she had known Mormor for years and they were here to announce that they *weren't* a couple. But still.

'Mormor loves you,' Jannes said. 'You know that.'

Well, Lara certainly loved Mormor, that much was true. She was mischievous and sharp and wry. And Lara still hadn't quite got the knack of knowing if she was one hundred per cent joking or not at any time. But she still couldn't shake these nerves.

'Hmm, we'll see if she still feels that way about me when she finds out I'm not really making an honest man out of you.'

'She doesn't think that we're getting married. It's not that far out of hand.'

Lara shuddered at the thought of things between her and Jannes getting that far—the certainty that she would end up losing him if they did.

'Well, that's a relief at least.'

'Ready?' Jannes asked, and then knocked on the door. Lara set her shoulders, not sure why she felt as if she were going into battle.

'Älskling!' Mormor announced, throwing open the door. 'And you brought Lara with you. You're a good boy.'

She pinched his cheek and Lara smothered

a laugh at the grimace on Jannes's face. 'You two have made an old woman very happy. I knew you couldn't be so stupid for ever. I can't believe it's taken you so long to work out that you're perfect for one another.'

Jannes threw Lara a look that was pure *I told you so* as they walked through the apartment to the elegant living room.

'Like I explained on the phone, Mormor,' Jannes said, his voice slow and deliberate. 'Lara and I are just friends. We were pretending to be a couple for…for a few reasons, but we're not really together.'

Mormor narrowed her eyes at him. 'I saw a picture of you kissing her. Are you telling me you go around kissing women who are not your girlfriend?'

Well, that sent him a delightful shade of pink, Lara thought, watching him squirm with embarrassment.

'Like I keep saying, that wasn't real.'

'I imagined it? I didn't see you kiss? Are you trying to make me think I'm going senile?'

'No, of course not. We did kiss, but—'

'So you are friends who kiss sometimes. She is your girlfriend,' Mormor declared, as if that settled the matter. 'Now, Lara, I need you to tell me everything and explain in great detail because Jannes has told me nothing.' She tutted and Lara felt a lurch of dread in her stomach.

'Mormor,' Lara said as they followed Mormor through to the kitchen, watched her fill a coffee pot from the tap and add heaped scoops of coffee. 'I'm really not his girlfriend. I'm sorry if we've disappointed you.'

'Oh, you kids, always overcomplicating things.' Mormor threw her hands up in an expression of exasperation as she reached into a high cupboard for cups and saucers. 'Jannes. If I say she's your girlfriend, she's your girlfriend. Now, who is going to drink coffee with me?'

'Some help you were,' Jannes said under his breath as Mormor bustled around them, taking a tin of cinnamon buns from the cupboard and swearing colourfully when she couldn't find the milk jug.

'I told her!' Lara whispered back. 'It's not my fault she didn't want to listen.'

'No, you're right,' Jannes said, shaking his head, the picture of dejection. 'It's my fault for yesterday. For thinking that something like this would be simple.'

She hated when Jannes looked dejected. It just made her want to comfort him. To make him feel better. In all sorts of ways that would lead to nothing but trouble for them both. So she kept things on track.

'It's your fault for thinking that you know better than Mormor whether I'm your girl-friend? I don't think you can really take the blame for that. So what do we do?' They threw a look over to Mormor, where she was arranging the coffee things on a silver tray on the kitchen island.

'We drink the coffee and eat the pastries, I suppose,' he said. 'Try and show her that she's made a mistake.'

Lara crossed her arms in front of her body. 'How do we prove that we're not together? It's not like we would be going at it on the kitchen counter either way.'

He spluttered in surprise and Lara laughed. 'Oh, close your mouth, Jannes,' she whispered. 'You're so easily shocked. It makes it impossible not to tease you. You're adorable.'

He threw a look to make sure Mormor

wasn't listening and then crossed his arms and leaned back against the wall. 'Adorable?'

'You still have a problem with adorable?' Lara asked with a smile.

'It's not very manly.'

'Ah—' She laughed quietly '—and you want to impress me with your manliness?'

'Stop flirting, you two,' Mormor interrupted, lifting up the tray with an ominous clinking of china. 'Anyone would think you are boyfriend and girlfriend.'

'We weren't flirting,' Jannes and Lara protested together.

'Right, and the Pope doesn't wear a hat,' Mormor said. 'Enough talking anyway. Jannes, I need your help in the kitchen. Lara, make yourself at home, my dear. I'll have your man back to you in a moment.'

'I'm not—'

'He's not—'

'How can you just refuse to believe two people who say they're not together?' Jannes asked in the car later, for what felt like the millionth time. He was pinching the bridge of his nose in that way he always did when he was tired, and it was reassuring to know that she wasn't the only one feeling the after-effects of their late-night *Love Island* binge. It had been gone two o'clock when she had finally given in to sleep.

'If anyone is up to the task it's Mormor. Do you think she really didn't believe us or was she just winding us up?'

'I don't know how you cannot believe it when you have the both of us there telling her we made the whole thing up.'

Lara nodded; she'd been thinking the same thing. 'So she's winding us up. Any idea why, other than to torture us?'

'Honestly, when it comes to Mormor it's anyone's guess. So…what do you think?'

'What do I think about what?'

Jannes gestured to her, and them himself. 'About this whole dating thing. Fake dating.'

'I don't really get where this is going, Jannes.'

'I was just wondering if it's something that you're still happy to continue,' he said, looking a little awkward. He looked it; she felt it. She wasn't sure that this was at all a good idea.

'Even after all this with Mormor?' she asked, going for the easy excuse, the one

that didn't give away too much about what
she felt.

'She's clearly going to believe whatever
she wants, regardless of what we say or do,'
Jannes said. 'So maybe we should just do
what's best for us.'

She raised an eyebrow. 'And you're still
sure that's pretending to date?'

'Well, you have all those family things
that you were invited to at the wedding. The
twins' christening is soon, isn't it? And the
longer that we appear together the better it is
for my chances of securing sponsorship. Just
one appearance with you has generated more
positive press than I've had in a year.'

'I'm pretty sure that was your doing, with
the special achievement award,' Lara pointed
out. He had earned that award, and she didn't
want him thinking that his successes were
down to anything but his own hard work. She
couldn't take the claim for that.

'And I think it's because everyone adores
you and they have to like me when I'm near
you.'

She shook her head. 'So you're just using
me for my adorability?'

'No, we're helping each other out. But I'm

not going to push you into anything you don't want to do. If it makes you uncomfortable, we won't do it. It's as simple as that. I don't want to do anything that risks our friendship.'

Their friendship. Which they had to protect at all costs, because if they lost sight of that at the wrong moment then she was sure that they would do something stupid that would mean that she lost him for ever. And then they would both end up hurt, and broken, and without their best friend there to hand out tissues and help pick up the pieces. She couldn't bear the thought of having to go through something like that without Jannes there in her corner. Or the thought of hurting Jannes, and then not being the one to hold him and help him heal.

'You *are* my friend, Jannes, and all the hand-holding and kissing and stuff, that's not important, is it? We know what we are to each other, and what we're not. And as long as we remember that then the other stuff doesn't matter. This just makes our lives a little easier, with no cost.'

'And when we're not in public then nothing changes,' Jannes assured her. 'We carry on as before. We're friends, Lara. Nothing's going to change that.'

Good, because she didn't want to back out of this now. Later that night, as they tucked into a takeaway, she thought again about the family events she'd agreed to go to, and how she couldn't even consider going without Jannes at her side. And it didn't cost her anything to show up to Jannes's events. It took dating completely off her radar, meant that she could concentrate on her work, her studying…and not on those commitment issues Jannes always seemed to want to make her talk about. It was hard not to think about those issues when she was with her family, faced with the evidence of how little she had meant to her father. How she had been a footnote to his real life. How easy she had been to hurt. How destructive following his desires had been for the two families that he'd destroyed.

With Jannes by her side, it had all felt… less bleak. She'd felt less disposable. Sure, it helped that no one was asking her about her love life any more, but it helped that he was simply there. Grounding her. Reminding her that she was present and she mattered.

'Okay,' she said at last. 'We'll keep things going a little longer. If you're sure you wouldn't rather be dating someone else for real.'

'I'm sure,' he told her, and she took comfort from the certainty in his voice.

'And are you sure you don't want to talk about that?' she pushed him. 'We're friends, Jannes. I don't like the thought that you're missing out on meeting someone for real because you're sitting through family parties with me.'

'I... I wouldn't be dating anyway,' he told her.

She tried to keep her voice light, as if the idea of talking with Jannes about his love life wasn't giving her butterflies. 'Oh?'

He shrugged. 'I haven't dated for a while. You hadn't noticed?'

Well, of course she'd *noticed*. She couldn't help but notice that it had been over a year since she'd seen him with anyone else.

'I noticed. Why is that, though? You can't be short of offers.'

He picked up his chopsticks and dug them into his Pad Thai, not meeting her eyes. 'I just didn't see the point, after a while. I didn't want—don't want—anything serious, and after a while the casual thing gets repetitive, don't you think?'

Yeah, it did, which was precisely why she'd stopped doing it too. But she knew it was more than that. That he was scared of getting hurt. Of having someone walk away from him the way his parents had done, over and over again. She couldn't trust herself to never do that to him, never to hurt him, and that meant she had to hide what she really felt.

'You're not worried that I'm going to be getting in your way?' Jannes asked, with the honesty that she loved him for.

She shrugged. 'I'm not missing much. Not when I already know that it's not going anywhere—not when I'll freak out and leave as soon as the question of whether I can trust him comes up.' In the end she'd realised that it was far simpler not to get into something, rather than walking in while simultaneously checking for a secure exit. She would have thought that Jannes would have understood that better than anyone. But they'd never actually talked about this before.

'Why doesn't it ever work out?' he asked. 'Why don't you want it to?'

'Because I can't make it work,' Lara said, her voice tightening slightly as she defended herself. She didn't expect this from Jannes. More than anyone, he was supposed to understand. 'Because, at the back of my mind, I'm always wondering if they're going home to someone else every time I say goodbye. It's just easier not to start something; isn't that basically what you just told me about why you don't date?'

'I don't know; it just seems…sadder when we're talking about you.'

'Ouch,' she said, leaning away from him.

'No—' he dropped his chopsticks and reached for her hand '—I don't mean that you're sad. I just don't like the idea that you've given up because you haven't found a guy who you know will treat you like you deserve. You're amazing and any guy should feel incredibly lucky to have you.'

She rolled her eyes at him. 'You're patronising me.' After all, it wasn't as if he was pushing for the chance to be with her for real. He was quite clear that faking it was all that was ever going to be on offer from him. Which was fine. Obviously.

'I'm sorry. That wasn't my intention,' he

apologised, and then hesitated. 'This is all to do with your dad, right?' he asked.

It was as if he had thrown cold water over her, killing the conversation dead. 'Jannes. I really don't want to talk about my father with you. I'm happy fake dating and so are you. I won't grill you on your reasons; you don't grill me on mine. I thought that was the deal?'

'Okay, fine,' Jannes said at last. 'But if it's not working for you, you have to tell me and we just undo the whole arrangement. Okay?'

'Fine.'

She picked up her chopsticks, heaped more Pad Thai on her plate, and then chewed on a dumpling thoughtfully and sank back into the sofa cushions. 'So what do we do next?' she asked, trying to steer the conversation onto safer ground. 'Should we compare diaries? I've already had invitations for some of the family stuff you agreed to at Pip's wedding. It's only a month until the twins' christening.'

'Fine, yes, I suppose we should. I'll forward you details of a few things. The regatta in Harbourside is happening in a couple of weeks. I'll be there meeting with potential sponsors—it would be good if you could be there, help the image, you know, if you're there doing the girlfriend thing. And I think you'll enjoy it.'

She nodded. 'Okay. Regatta in a couple of weeks.'

'And of course I have a spare room at my place there so we don't have to repeat the *only one bed* incident.'

'I didn't realise it had been so traumatic for you,' she said with an exaggerated head-tilt. 'Poor little flower.'

He shoved her playfully with his foot. 'It wasn't traumatic; it just complicates things, doesn't it?'

CHAPTER NINE

LARA PUT ON a wide-brimmed sunhat as she stepped out of her car. With the air-con on all the way down from London, she hadn't realised how hot the day had become.

Jannes had warned her that he wouldn't be there when she arrived and so she followed the instructions he'd sent her to get into the key safe. She hadn't seen his Harbourside house before. He visited Mormor so often that he had a room there, and it made more sense for them to meet up in London and hang out at her place. Which meant that she had never seen a space that was entirely Jannes's. She couldn't help but be secretly pleased that he couldn't meet her until later. It gave her a chance to see his place without him in it. She wasn't sure why exactly that appealed so much: if there was something she wanted to know about him then she could just ask.

But this was different, she thought.

The hallway was bright and clean and sparse, with just a couple of pairs of shoes stored neatly by the door, a couple of jackets she recognised on the hooks. She dropped the key into a bowl on the shelf above the radiator and walked through to the kitchen. Ah, so here was Jannes. Glass doors covered the whole of the back of the house, offering unbroken views of the sea, all the way out to the horizon. A host of boats bobbed in the water, sails billowing in the breeze, and she wondered how often Jannes sat here, watching people out on the water. Every seat in the open-plan room—from the great big corner sofa to the pale wood chairs arranged around a circular table—faced towards the sea.

And there were touches of the ocean inside too: the woven blanket tossed haphazardly on the sofa, with a mix of blues and greens, aquas and azures, and sky and stormy grey. The artwork on the walls all captured a part of life on the shore or the sea: shells, and fishing boats, and always the rich blue-green of deep water.

She wandered along the bookshelves that held Jannes's trophies and, across the facing wall, the ones with actual books. She pulled a few out and looked at the titles, curious. There were books on travel and nature and woodwork. Sports biographies and sailing, and more sailing, of course.

She walked back through to the kitchen and found the coffee machine, made herself a double espresso and slid the glass doors open. A wide deck spanned the width of the house, with a glass barrier the only thing breaking the view from the deck to the sea. Lara sat on a wicker chair, eyes drawn to the white caps and sunlight glinting on the water and felt the stress and anxiety of her working week fall away. She could get used to this. Well, maybe she would, she considered, depending on how long she and Jannes kept up their pretence.

She watched the yachts out on the water and listened to the rattle of wires in masts from the marina. With every lungful of sea air, her body felt looser and heavier. If Jannes didn't call soon and let her know that his meeting was finished then she might decide that she was never leaving this deck.

As if on cue, her phone buzzed in her pocket. Jannes. She hit answer and tried to hide the smile in her voice.

'All done schmoozing?' she asked.

'For now. If you want to join me here, we can do some more together if you like. You know you're much more charming than I am.'

'Sure,' she said, stretching out in the chair. If she didn't move soon she would definitely fall asleep here. 'I need to earn my keep.'

She could practically hear his frown. 'You know that's not what I meant.'

'I know. I'm kidding.' It was adorable, how seriously he took her sometimes.

'I'll walk back up and meet you. Shouldn't take more than ten minutes if you're ready to head out.'

'I am, but there's no need to walk back up here. I'll mooch through the town and meet you at the yacht club,' she told him. She'd never visited Harbourside before, and wanted to explore in her own time.

She said goodbye, pulled the glass doors closed and gathered up her bag and her sunglasses and hat. Pocketing the key, she pulled the door closed behind her and followed Jannes's directions to the main street of the town. Bunting was strung between the shops, across the cobbled street, and the sun was fierce on the heads and shoulders of pinkened tourists.

Ahead of her, a toddler sat down abruptly, striped pinafore dress gathering around her chunky legs as she sobbed and declared she wouldn't walk another step. Lara gave the parents a smile as she passed the family, and stopped to look in the window of a boutique. There was vintage furniture, clothes and jewellery of all her Instagram dreams. She took a couple of photos through the window and made a mental note to stop in before she went back to London. The next window was filled with second-hand books, and if it wasn't for the knowledge that Jannes was waiting for her at the entrance of the marina she was in danger of losing the whole afternoon in the little row of independent shops that led down to the seafront.

She followed the sound of the music and found Jannes waiting for her by the entrance to the marina, ice cream melting down his wrist.

She laughed as he licked a trickle of cream that was making its way around the circle of his wrist bone. Laughter was definitely the right response to that, she told herself, eyes still fixed on his wrist. She definitely shouldn't offer to lick it off for him. She licked her lips involuntarily as he held the cone out to her.

'I got you ice cream. Probably should have waited until you were actually here.'

'You're sweet,' she said, reaching up to press a kiss to his cheek, just a friendly thing to do, and took the ice cream from him.

'How are things going?' she asked as they walked down steps into the marina and along the row of yachts moored there. She tucked a free strand of hair behind her ear before it got stuck in the ice cream.

'Not bad,' Jannes said, slipping his hands in his pockets as they walked. His sunglasses hid his eyes, making it hard to read his expression. She was distracted, anyway, by the glint of sunlight on the pale hair on the back of his legs, bare skin between his shorts and his deck shoes.

'Lara?'

'Hmm, what was that?' She tried to cover her embarrassment, not sure how long she'd been distracted.

'Nothing—I just asked you if you found the house okay. I'm sorry I wasn't there when you arrived but they changed the meeting at the last minute.'

'Like I said on the phone, it was absolutely fine. And I love the house. You do know you might never get rid of me now? I think I could live here for ever.'

Even with the sunglasses on there was no hiding the flash of panic across Jannes's face. 'I was kidding, Jannes. I'm not really about to move in.'

'I didn't panic.'

'You look terrified.'

'It's fine.'

'I do know what we're doing here, and I know that moving in with you isn't a part of it. I just meant that I love the house. You need to stop freaking out every time that something I say makes you think I'm trying to trap you into committing to me. We're not even together. I don't understand why you keep thinking I'm trying to make you do something you don't want to do. This was *your idea*.'

Because if he started to think that she might stay, then he had to be afraid that she might leave. It didn't make any sense, of course it didn't. He knew that they weren't really dating. Knew that her trip to his home was part of their charade and nothing more. But irrational fears were just that—irrational. And any time that he got the feeling that Lara might want to stay, might want to make this thing more than a fantasy, he got this feeling like a hook in his gut, a wrench, an inkling of what it might feel like when she would inevitably leave him, and he couldn't help but retreat.

He'd been here before. He knew he threw up these walls and barriers when he liked someone too much. It had destroyed relationships before, and he was determined that this wasn't going to come between him and Lara. If he was willing to risk that, then he wouldn't be so sure that fake dating was the only romantic future that was available to them.

'Jannes!' he heard shouted by someone in the crowd of people outside the yacht club, and he turned to see his agent walking towards him. Lara slipped her hand into his. She didn't break her stride or even look up at him, just gave him this little show of togetherness as though it was nothing.

He had to keep his head on the job here,

which was securing sponsorship for his next transatlantic race. Otherwise, the three months he had pencilled in for the race next season started to stretch uncomfortably in front of him. Standing still always felt like this. He had learned as a kid that it was a lot less painful to tell himself that he was racing back to school for extra training than because it was better to walk away than be left somewhere. When he had signed up for every sports club and extracurricular activity, he had told himself that he was just a sporty kind of guy, not that he couldn't bear the thought of sitting with nothing but his own thoughts to distract him.

'Lara, lovely to see you again,' Chris, Jannes's agent, said, looking a little surprised to see her with him. Jannes rolled his eyes—was it so out of character that he turned up with the same girl twice? Okay, stupid question. But Chris was only giving him that look because of the bad press he'd been getting before this thing with Lara, and every word of those articles had been fictional. He had wanted to deny it publicly but, according to his manager, that would just add fuel to the fire, and now his career was at risk because his sponsors weren't happy. He loved his job, but it came with a cost—and this was it. He would be happy if he never had to take another meeting with a sponsor again. But, unless he happened to find a spare few million to fund his ocean-going lifestyle, he couldn't see that happening any time soon.

Chris dragged them over to meet Spencer, the representative from a new online bank who were looking to raise their profile with sponsorship, and within half a minute of him introducing Lara she had them charmed and eating out of her hand. It was always that way with her—she was so disarmingly friendly that it was impossible not to fall in love with her.

He remembered the first time he'd met her, at a party thrown by a sportswear brand. When she'd walked up to him with a tray of canapés she'd swiped from the wait staff, and had asked him if he was as bored as she was. She had suggested that they help out the servers to liven things up a bit. By the end of the night they'd been firm friends, and if he had known one thing it was that he wanted her in his life. Which put to bed any temptation he had felt to see if it could go further. Dating

her would be a fast track to alienating her—
he knew his limitations. He knew the damage
that he carried around inside himself, and the
harm that could do to others if they got too
close. Hurting himself by taking a risk was
unappealing. Hurting Lara was unthinkable.

He loved to watch her in action at events
like this—her complete lack of social nice-
ties, which translated into charm rather than
rudeness. If anyone else said half the things
that she did, they'd be met with stony silence.
And yet Lara always managed to cultivate a
circle of guffaws that followed her around a
party. He could always locate her by listening for the most outraged laughter.

Spencer was not immune to her charms,
it seemed. Lara was listening with rapt attention as he explained the features of his
new banking app—a subject Jannes knew
she wasn't the least bit interested in. And all
the time that she was nodding along and asking probing questions, she never once let go
of his hand. It shouldn't be the part of this
that was holding his attention—and yet there
was something about her warm palm pressing against his that had shut off key operat-
ing pathways in his brain.

He snapped back to attention when he heard mention of the transatlantic record attempt, and he looked from Spencer to Lara, trying to catch up with the conversation.

'Lara was just telling me your plans for next summer. You've got your eye on that speed record, eh?'

'Well, he's already the youngest to cross single-handed and the youngest to skipper a circumnavigation,' Lara said without hesitation. 'I keep telling him to leave some records for somebody else, but he doesn't listen to me.'

'Well, I like your ambition,' Spencer said. But Jannes was having difficulty looking away from Lara, or from ignoring the swelling in his chest he felt hearing her list his achievements. He hadn't known she'd been paying that much attention to what he'd been up to—they rarely spoke about work. 'And I know there's an issue with the press coverage. Sorry to bring it up—' he slid an apologetic look to Lara '—but you seem like a solid sort of chap to me.'

Which had to be entirely Lara's doing, Jannes knew, mainly because he had barely managed to get a word in the entire conversation.

'I'm not making any promises, of course,' Spencer went on. 'But I think that Chris and I have a lot to talk about.'

Jannes looked at Lara as Spencer walked away. 'How do you do that?' he asked her, mouth agape.

'What?' she asked with a bewildered smile.

'Charm people like that?' Jannes said. 'He would have given you anything you asked for.'

'I don't know.' She shrugged. 'I listen. I talk. I'm honest.'

It was more than that. There was just something about Lara that was so easy to fall in love with. In a friendly way, he reminded himself, spotting the way that his thoughts were heading. He had only fallen in love with her in a friendly way. 'You know,' he observed lightly, 'not everyone likes honesty.'

'They do with me,' Lara said with another smile, but narrowing her eyes at him.

'I know. I noticed that. I'm wondering how we bottle that and sell it so you can be my next sponsor.'

She laughed, and Jannes breathed a sigh of relief that they had swum out of deeper waters, for now, anyway.

'Well, if you figure it out, let me know. I think I could stand being a billionaire, as an entirely selfless act, of course. So, do you have any more meetings, or shall we go have fun?'

'Why does it always make me nervous when you say things like that?'

'Because of the high probability of me stealing a yacht?'

He shook his head. 'Oh, God, Lara, please don't steal a yacht. If you want one, there are half a dozen people here who would probably just give you one for free.'

'Should we try?' Her eyes lit up, and he couldn't resist teasing her.

'If you like. Do you get a lot of yachting opportunities in Hackney?'

'You're such a killjoy. And also annoyingly right,' she said. 'So maybe I should steal a really big yacht and just live in it here.'

Jannes shook his head. 'Come on,' he said, pulling her gently by the hand.

'Where are we going?'

'Window shopping.'

He led her down to the water, and along the jetty to where a long line of boats was moored, from the little dinghies the kids from the yacht club sailed to huge pleasure cruisers with their satellite masts, multiple decks and speedboats at the aft deck.

'What are we doing?' Lara asked again, grabbing hard onto his arm and nearly toppling them into the water as they stepped down onto the floating pontoon.

'Woah, you all right there?' he asked, grabbing her and pulling her towards him to steady her.

'Didn't realise I'd need my sea legs just yet,' she said, and they both laughed. But his laughter died quickly when he realised how close he had pulled her to stop her falling. They hadn't been this close since that night in Liverpool. He'd had to forcibly remove memories of it from his brain. How her high heels had tipped her forward so her hips had brushed his thighs, her breasts just barely touching his ribcage. The way she'd tilted her chin up so that she could meet his gaze, despite the difference in height between them.

He was forcibly reminded of standing not unlike this at Pip's wedding, with Lara's forehead resting against his chest and his hands in her hair. He reached for a strand of it now, tweaking the end of a curl where it tickled against his hand. This was where they always pulled away. Pretended that neither of them had noticed the sparks flying between them. He never asked if Lara had felt them too. That hadn't seemed necessary, considering he had no intention of acting on them. But now that they had blurred the lines between friendship and something more, it was hard not to wonder whether she felt the same. He could just ask her. He probably should just ask her—get it out in the open. Take the mystery and the danger out of it.

Except he wasn't sure that he wanted to talk about it. If it turned out he was imagining this—and he had no intention of acting on any of it—it would just be stirring things up for no reason. He just had to do what he always did when he had these thoughts—push them as deep down as possible and focus on something else.

'So you're in the market for a yacht,' he said, getting his mind out on the water, where it was safer.

'Absolutely.' She threaded her arm through his and looked at him conspiratorially as they walked. 'How do I do this? Do I just pick the biggest one?'

'That's one approach.' He rolled his eyes. 'Or, you know, you think about which features are most important to you and how each vessel measures up, and the environmental credentials of each company and—'

'Maybe one of the huge ones that has a little speedboat on the back. That seems practical. A boat for every mood. Or I could just pick the most expensive one. Or the cleanest or the shiniest. I like the idea of the cleanest one.'

'What if you liked one of the others better, though, and then we just took a pressure washer to it?'

Lara sighed melodramatically. 'Darling, you are making this far too complicated.'

A cannon sounded, marking the start of a race, but Lara startled, making the pontoon wobble again. Jannes pulled her tighter against him and wrapped an arm around her waist.

'Should we get you back on dry land?' he asked.

'That's an excellent idea. Window shopping makes me thirsty. And I'm pretty sure you owe me a G&T. Photos first, though,' she said, holding out her phone. 'You're an

Instagram boyfriend now. Got to start acting like one.'

He took the phone from her and took a few pictures of her posing in front of the yachts, capturing her hair whipping in the wind and her shrieks of laughter as the pontoon wobbled and she nearly lost her footing again. She looked beautiful, of course. He wasn't sure there was anything even he could do to a camera that would prevent that.

'Really?' he asked, scrolling through the pictures so that she could see them. 'I still need to hear why it is I owe you a drink.'

'Well, I'm pretty sure I just locked in that sponsorship for you. And I drove all the way down here and was nearly lost at sea.'

He laughed. 'You're impossible.'

'It's why you love me.'

The worst thing about it was that she was right. He'd had to acknowledge to himself a long time ago that he loved her. Platonically, of course. Everybody loved their friends. And yes, the fact that he was wildly attracted to her could make that complicated—if he let it—so he just wouldn't. It was as simple as that. If he wanted her in his life, he had to make sure he kept things safe. And friendship was safe. Anything more intense risked both of them getting hurt. And he didn't want to hurt Lara any more than he could bear the thought of Lara realising he wasn't worth sticking around for and leaving.

He left Lara outside the yacht club, where she instantly entered into conversation with a couple who had crewed for him last year, and with whom she seemed to have struck up an instant friendship. When he returned, clutching two balloon glasses of gin and tonic, Lara was in hysterics, wiping her eyes, and looking instantly guilty when she spotted Jannes coming towards her.

'Why do I get the feeling you were talking about me?' he asked.

'They were just telling me what a tyrant you are.' Lara laughed. 'How have I never seen this side of you?'

He raised an eyebrow at the two crew.

'Tyrant seems a little harsh. I'm…competitive.'

They all fell into hysterical laughter again and he decided he'd rather not know the specifics of what had been said in his absence.

'Have you seen much of Harbourside?' one of them asked Lara, and she shook her head.

'So far just the yacht club and Jannes's place. I'm looking forward to exploring.'

'Well, if you ever want to get together... No, what am I saying? Of course you don't. Just call me in a year or two when you're out of the honeymoon phase.'

Jannes hadn't realised until he caught their pointed looks that his arm had sneaked back around Lara's waist, as if it always rested there. He met Lara's eyes and the expression there hit him somewhere in the gut, the top of his ears turning pink as he wondered whether his thoughts were as clear on his face as Lara's were on hers.

'You two are too cute,' one of the crew said. 'Don't let him get away.'

Lara nodded solemnly. 'He's a dictator but he's one of the benevolent ones.'

'Well, thank you for that resounding review,' Jannes said with a laugh, 'but I'm going to have to steal Lara away before you spill all my secrets.'

'Everyone is so nice,' Lara exclaimed as they walked back to his house that evening, the light fading from the sky and the sounds of the party still going on in the yacht club behind them.

'I've told you before,' Jannes said as they skirted round the side of his house and came straight out on to the deck behind, with its view of the stars reflecting on the water. 'You have that effect on people—they're never half so nice to me.'

'Because they're in awe of you.'

He scoffed, but she tugged on his hand to pull him closer.

'I'm serious,' she said, meeting his eyes and fixing him there with a look. 'They respect you, and it's obvious why. I like seeing you here, you know. You make sense here in a way you don't in London.'

He huffed out a half-laugh. 'You do know it's quite hard not to be offended by that, considering you have only ever seen me in London before today. Which basically means I have never made sense to you.'

Lara smiled. 'What can I say—you're an enigma. Very mysterious. Impossible to know what you're thinking.'

Her voice had started out jokey, playful, but fell towards the end as her gaze dropped to his mouth and stayed there.

'Do you really want to know what I'm thinking?' he said. 'You only have to ask.'

But he wasn't sure that he wanted her to. He knew what he wanted the answer to be. He needed her to be sensible here, because he wasn't sure that he could count on himself to be. He was watching her mouth now, as intently as she had been watching his.

'Okay,' she said, her voice rough. 'What are you thinking about?'

'You.'

The word slipped out before he could stop it. The monosyllable the only sound he could manage amidst the cascade of malfunctions in his brain at the thought that she wasn't being careful with him.

'That's a coincidence,' Lara said, her voice dropping to something low and breathy and unfamiliar. 'I'm thinking about you too. Specifically, I'm thinking about kissing you. Does that freak you out?'

This was such a bad idea. This was everything that they had both been fighting for three years. Fighting harder than ever since that day in the park when they'd both discovered that the two of them together would be every bit as intensely perfect as he had always imagined it would be.

'Yes, it freaks me out,' he replied, too on

edge to smile. But he was so tired of fighting something that he knew would feel so right. All his life, he had watched people walk away from him. He'd nursed those wounds through his whole childhood. And here was something *good*. Someone who loved him and had never walked away and had never hurt him. And he didn't know if he could trust yet that that would never change, but he couldn't carry on pretending that she wasn't everything to him.

'I don't think that you should let that stop you though,' he added at last, his gaze fixed on her.

'From thinking about it or doing it?' she asked.

'Either.'

She narrowed her eyes at him. 'We agreed that it would be a bad idea. It would complicate things.'

He nodded. They had, but he couldn't bring himself to care right at this minute. 'Things are already complicated,' he told her. 'I can't stop thinking about you. About us together. I've never felt like this before, and I don't know what to do with that. This whole thing is complicated and I don't have the answers.'

'You've been thinking about it too?'

He shook his head. 'Jesus, Lara. Only every second since that day in London Fields.'

'That does sound complicated.' She nodded thoughtfully, her eyes still fixed on his mouth, and he wondered if she was ever going to put him out of his misery.

And then, finally, after all the months and years of resisting this, he was done. He was out. He couldn't do it any longer. 'You're killing me here. Are you kissing me or not?'

Finally, she broke into a smile. 'Not, if you're not going to ask nicely,' she said, even as her hands landed on his waist.

He let out a growl of frustration, grabbed her by the hips and pulled her closer, tipping up her chin with one hand so that he didn't have to break eye contact. 'I can be nice.'

She nipped at his finger with her teeth. 'I've changed my mind. Nice is overrated.'

She pulled him down with a hand on the nape of his neck and rested their foreheads together for a breath, and then another.

He was braced for the feel of her, his body tense, but the kiss, when it came, was so gentle that he melted instantly. Her body sank into his as he wrapped both arms around her waist, pulling her up towards him so that he could chase her lips before they ghosted away.

He breathed in her scent as he gathered her close, nudging at her nose with his, tipping her face up so she could kiss him deeper. When she moaned into his mouth, he thought he might die. Or explode. Die then explode, explode then die. He didn't know or care. All he knew was that he wanted more. More of this. More of her. More of her lips hungry against his and her tongue flickering into his mouth. More of her arching back against the hard brace of his arms.

They had nowhere to hide this time. No excuses. No pretending that this was somehow for show, or for other people, or for whatever reason *not real*. This was just them, acting on the instincts they'd been fighting for years. Years. He pulled away abruptly. They'd fought this. For good reason.

'Freaking out?' Lara asked, and she was so out of breath it made him want to kiss her again.

Instead, he nodded. 'Yes. You?'

'Oh, yeah. Shall we make it hard to think again?'

He threaded his fingers in her hair and kissed her again, aware of nothing but the taste and the smell and the *feel* of her. Every fantasy of the last weeks…months, years, coming alive in his hands.

A boom overhead pulled them apart and he looked up to see a shower of colourful sparks falling to earth.

'Fireworks,' Lara breathed, looking up. 'Think the universe is trying to tell us something?'

'Just trying to tell us it's the last day of the regatta,' Jannes said, breathing heavily and looking for reason.

Lara slapped his chest gently. 'Killjoy.'

'Sorry,' he said, looking directly at her and meeting her gaze for the first time in this new world. 'We should probably talk about what just happened,' he went on, real life starting to creep in at the edges of whatever this thing was.

'I know. We should,' Lara said, holding his gaze until another boom behind her made her jump. 'After the fireworks?'

He nodded and she turned in his arms, leaning back against him and watching the fireworks over the water, explosions in blue and green and red. In blinding white. He kissed the side of her neck, his fingertips exploring her collarbone, down the side of her arm, his hand circling her wrist and then back up to just behind her ear. Later, they would talk about this. They would remind each other about all the reasons they'd agreed that they didn't want to do this. All the ways that they could get hurt, and the reasons why they couldn't let that happen.

Later—tomorrow—they would talk themselves out of it. Undo this step and get their friendship back. But, for this moment, he didn't have to pretend not to want her. It was only in release that he realised how heavy this had been to carry. Only when he gave in that he could feel how hard he had been fighting. Only in kissing Lara—no tricks, no pretence—that he could feel how desperately right it was. Giving in was so much easier. It was as natural as breathing. His body welcomed it and his mind quieted at having her in his arms.

And while he was watching the fireworks he could just soak her in. Absorb how right this felt without worrying about the consequences. He squeezed tight around her waist—unwilling to waste a second of this time before they had to get back to real life.

Lara's hands covered his, fingers threading together to hold her even tighter, and her head fell back against his chest, giving him a clear view down her elegant neck, over flawless shoulders and collarbones, the freckled skin of her chest and the shadows of her cleavage. He let his face fall against the side of hers, the luminosity of her skin a greater draw than the lights in the sky.

He pressed his lips against her cheek and felt a knot tightening in his belly when she let her head fall to the side, baring more skin, opening up a path for him to kiss down to her pulse spot, letting his lips pause there to feel the steady thud. From there he found the sensitive spot where her neck met shoulder, letting his lips pause as she sighed, untangled a hand from his and let it come up to cup the back of his head. Her fingertips played with the short hairs at the nape of his neck, and she moaned quietly when he shivered under her fingers. When one of his hands found the soft skin of her stomach she turned in his embrace, her arms winding around his neck, pulling herself higher, pressing her body hard against his, and the fireworks ceased to exist. The sky and the moon and the stars ceased to exist. There was just Lara at the centre of his universe, and it was the first time the world had felt right.

He pulled away, breathless, and watched Lara as her breathing gradually slowed and eyes flickered open. She glanced over her shoulder. 'Fireworks have finished,' she said.

'Regatta's over.'

Untangling her arms from around his neck, she let herself fall back onto her heels, introducing just a whisper of space between them.

'Are we going to forget about this?' she asked.

'I'm not sure I can forget.' But his face was hard and closing fast. He might not be able to forget, but that didn't mean that he thought this had been a good idea. That he wanted to repeat it.

'We pretend then,' she said, making the call for both of them. 'We go back to how things have always been and pretend that this never happened.'

'I don't want to lose you, Lara. You know how much I like—'

Like. Nice. These banalities were going to kill her one of these days. Of course they *liked* each other. If she liked him less, maybe she could countenance the idea of breaking his heart one day. But she loved him, and that meant that she couldn't be the one to hurt him. That he couldn't be the one that she hurt, trying to work out if the damage that her heart had sustained was permanent.

'I know. I don't want to lose you either,' she told him, the simplest version of what she was feeling.

'So you agree that this would be a bad idea?'

'I do. You know I do. But that doesn't mean I can't regret what I can't have.' She leant her forehead against him, because regret wasn't a strong enough word for what she was feeling. She wanted this to work. Every bone in her body ached, knowing that everything she wanted was just within reach, and she wasn't going to let herself grab it and hold it tight. She had to do this. If she wanted him in her life, she couldn't pretend to him that she wasn't damaged.

He tucked a strand of hair behind her ear. 'I'd hurt you, Lara. And I don't want to hurt you.' It was as if his heart was echoing directly from hers. But he had this all wrong.

She wasn't the one that was going to hurt; it was him. She trusted him, even if he didn't trust himself.

'I'm not scared of that,' she told him, even though it didn't change where this was going.

'But—'

'I'm not scared of you hurting me, Jannes. But that doesn't mean I want a relationship any more than you do. I've never been with someone without eventually pushing them away. You know that. I don't want that to happen to us.'

He nodded, and she listened to the thump of his heart for just a few seconds longer, knowing that she was going to have to step away if they wanted to save this friendship.

'I know,' he said, his voice echoing through his chest. 'So we agree. We pretend this didn't happen.'

She nodded, and finally lifted her head. 'If we're trying to forget it, though, I think we need to stop pretending we're together. This makes it too complicated—it will be too hard to ignore this feeling if we're holding hands and kissing and pretending in front of other people.'

He let his arms drop from around her waist,

and something inside her broke. Something she didn't realise could fracture any more than it already had. 'I agree. But I need to ask one last favour. A meeting with Spencer tomorrow morning. After that, you go back to London. Next time I come up it will be as if this never happened.'

He saw her swallow.

'Okay, it'll end tomorrow. And Mormor— you're going to talk to Mormor about this? Get her to stop meddling.'

'I'll deal with Mormor.'

She smiled, and he knew she was imagining how that conversation might go. 'I'm sorry I won't get to see that.'

One corner of his mouth lifted, but he couldn't bring himself to smile properly, not when he knew this was ending, when it had hardly begun. 'Come. It might help.'

She nodded thoughtfully. 'I should go to bed,' she said at last, and just the word *bed* on her lips had his heart beating faster again. If this was going to be over tomorrow anyway... No. It was going to be hard enough to forget a kiss. If they took this further there would be no going back. No way that they could pretend it had never happened. That would set him on a path that he wouldn't be able to leave until it reached its inevitable painful end.

'I'll show you to the guest room.'

At the door, she hesitated, fingers on the handle.

'Lara...'

'No, I'm not suggesting... Just...' she paused, and he couldn't help but hold his breath '...if it was going to be anyone, it would be you,' she said with a smile that managed to make her look sad.

He leaned in for a last kiss. Couldn't resist it. 'I wish things were different,' he said, leaning his forehead against hers, brushing his lips against hers. She broke the kiss, turning the door handle.

'Me too.'

CHAPTER TEN

LARA STARED AT the ceiling, wondering how long she'd been lying awake. A glance at the clock on her phone told her it was six a.m. Two hours then, since she'd woken from dreaming of Jannes and remembered how close they'd come last night to ruining their friendship. Waking frustrated and over-heated, she'd wondered how bad it would really be if she padded down the corridor and knocked on Jannes's door. And in less than a heartbeat she'd known the answer. It would be bad. Really bad, when they woke up and had to undo what they had done. So she'd tried to go back to sleep at first, and then, when she'd realised that wasn't going to happen, she had resigned herself to staring at the ceiling.

The sky started to lighten and she watched the sunrise, the expanse of the sea revealed more and more by the minute. Waiting for a new day to dawn and hoping that the sunshine would wash away the memories of last night. They just had to get through this one quick meeting and she could get back to London, away from whatever strange influences the sea air had had on them.

She heard Jannes walking past her door and was tempted to bury her head under the pillow. Maybe she should skip breakfast and just sneak back home. But they had resisted last night because they had wanted to protect one another—protect their friendship—and sneaking away at dawn wasn't going to make that happen. Would have the opposite effect, in fact. So she pulled an oversized cardigan on over her tank top and shorts and followed Jannes down the stairs.

'Morning,' she said, reaching the kitchen.

Jannes started, spinning on the spot and spilling his coffee. 'Gah,' he said, grabbing a tea towel and throwing it to the floor to mop up his spilt drink.

'I think the coffee's meant to go in your mouth,' Lara said, forcing a smile, trying to break the atmosphere.

'I'll work on that,' he said with a forced smile. 'I'll make another. Do you want one?'

'Of course,' Lara said, wondering what they had to do to break this awkwardness and get back to normal. That had been the whole point of stopping last night, when it had been the last thing she had wanted. If they had ruined their friendship anyway, she wished that she'd had less self-control.

'You going for a run?' she asked, eyes dropping to his shorts and running vest.

'Yeah. I thought I'd pick up breakfast on the way back. Pancakes? Waffles?'

'You're such a dreamboat.'

It was the sort of thing she'd been saying their whole friendship. A throwaway comment that would normally have raised a laugh and a frisson of sexual tension and which was forgotten a second later. This morning, it nearly made him drop a second cup of coffee. Whatever they had both said about not letting that kiss change things, it wasn't going to be as easy as just saying it and that making it true. They were going to have to work at it, she realised. Their friendship wasn't out of danger yet. It would be easy to let this awkwardness fester. To avoid one another for the next few weeks and have that turn into months and then years. They couldn't let that happen.

'Pancakes,' she said decisively. 'At least a dozen. Bacon, berries, syrup—the works. And whatever you're having.'

'You really know how to order. It's one of the best things about you.'

'Don't you forget it. Now, go for your run. I'll have coffee waiting when you get back.'

He hesitated at the door, and she knew that he was going to mention what had happened. But this conversation would be so much easier with coffee and pancakes in their bellies.

'Go. We'll talk when you get back. We're fine.' And she forced herself to give him a kiss on the cheek to prove it, though she wasn't sure which of them she was trying to convince more.

While he was out, she set the table with a pot of strong black coffee, a carton of orange juice she found at the back of the fridge, and plates and cutlery.

When Jannes returned, skin shining with sweat, she kept her gaze safely somewhere above his left ear.

'Shower!' she said, taking the takeaway

boxes from him, inhaling the scent of pancakes, bacon and maple syrup.

Jannes reappeared five minutes later, hair damp but less skin on show, and she forced a smile in his direction. 'Good run?' she asked, looking for a safe topic of conversation.

'Yeah,' Jannes replied. 'It's easier to think when I'm moving, you know.'

She took a deep breath. 'So we should talk about this, huh?'

'I'm not sure there's much to add from last night,' Jannes said, sitting at the table and opening the takeaway carton. 'You know how much I care about you. And you know how I feel about relationships. It's part of the reason this hasn't happened before, yes? And maybe we were stupid to think that we could just ignore it. But I don't think anything has changed to make this a good idea. I want you in my life. I don't want to hurt you.'

'I want that too. You know I don't do relationships either. But I don't agree that you would hurt me. And I'm not saying that because I want us to change our minds. I'm saying it because I'm your friend and it's upsetting that you would think that about yourself.'

'Then you have to trust me to know myself. I always leave. I don't know how to stay. Maybe if I wanted to change...'

She frowned at him. 'Don't you want to?'

'No. I'm sorry,' he added, and she knew her face must have fallen. 'Maybe I should, but it doesn't matter because I've tried before and I can't do it. It's just what happens—the minute I get too close to someone, the way I feel about them changes, and I just have to get away. I won't do that to you.'

Lara shook her head. 'I'm not asking you to. I just wonder if it's what you *want*.'

'Of course I don't want to be this broken, but that's beside the point.'

'Okay, well, I wasn't suggesting you should change, Jan. I just want you to be happy.'

'I *am* happy.'

'Fine.'

'Fine.'

They glared at each other for a moment, and then Jannes turned away, and she felt something fragile between them tear away. The fireworks of the night before suddenly felt like a distant memory.

'I have some emails I need to send before this meeting,' he said, standing and clearing the table. 'If you'd rather go straight back to London, I'd understand.'

'Jannes, no. You asked for my help. Of course I'll still come.'

He sighed, a long, sad sound. 'See? I'm doing it already. I'm messing things up in the process of trying to not mess things up.'

Lara fought for composure. 'Nothing's messed up, Jannes. We're a little awkward but we'll be fine. If I race off now, we'll only be saving up the awkwardness for the next time.'

'I'm sorry, Lara.' She thought for a moment that he was going to reach for her, but then that tension in his arms and his shoulders was gone, and they were further apart than ever.

'Don't be sorry. You seem to think you're denying me something that I want. You're not. You know that.'

'I do. But I still feel terrible.'

'I know. Me too.'

Jannes ordered them both coffee and glanced at his watch. Should he be worried that Spencer was ten minutes late? There was no point trying to second-guess it. Either he would sponsor him or he wouldn't. It was probably already too late to change his mind either way.

'Deep breaths,' Lara said, brushing her hand across his shoulder as she passed him on the way back from the bathroom. 'You're nervous,' she observed, sitting beside him and resting her arms on the table.

'Hmm...'

She pushed coffee in his direction, but he wasn't sure that more caffeine would help him feel more relaxed. Selfish though he knew it was, he just wanted her hand back on his shoulder. On any part of him, come to think of it. He'd woken up knowing that they had to set new boundaries after what had happened the night before. But that didn't mean that he wanted to.

Spencer turned up before he had a chance to worry about it further, and shook his hand with so much enthusiasm that for the first time Jannes let himself get his hopes up.

'Jannes, good to see you again. And Lara too. Congratulations, you sly pair! Why didn't you mention anything yesterday?'

Jannes glanced from Spencer to Lara, wondering if he was meant to know what he was talking about. But Lara looked as confused as Jannes felt.

'Erm, told you what, Spencer?' he asked,

hoping he wasn't making a mistake that might cost him his sponsorship.

'About the engagement! I saw the notice in *The Times* this morning. Well, I'm delighted for you both; that should go without saying.'

Jannes glanced across at Lara, who was hiding her shock well. Well enough that Jannes was sure that Spencer wouldn't spot it, but Jannes knew Lara better, and could see the hardness around her mouth and the tension in the usually fluid line of her shoulders.

'Could I just…?' Lara said, indicating the paper Spencer was holding.

'"Mr Jannes Henriksson and Ms Lara Hughes are delighted to announce their engagement",' Lara read.

She stayed silent for a moment, and Jannes could barely think, never mind speak.

'We…we're just surprised that they announced it already,' Lara said, and he thanked God she was thinking better on her feet than he was right now. 'We…um…we wanted to wait until we'd picked out a ring together,' she said, glancing at her left hand, and Jannes realised she was looking for and plugging the holes in their story.

Mormor. Mormor had to be behind this.

He would have to murder her. Or disown her. He couldn't believe... Actually, that wasn't strictly true. He could totally believe that she would do this. It hadn't been enough for her simply to not believe that they weren't really in a relationship—she had to up the ante and turn it into a fake engagement.

He glanced at Lara again. They had to brazen this out. He was so close to getting this funding. He took Lara's hand in his, startling her into looking up and meeting his gaze.

'I'm sorry, *älskling*,' he said, hoping that they would be able to muddle through this together, playing off each other's leads. 'I must have given them the wrong date. Good job we'd planned to choose your ring this afternoon.'

'Well, I'm delighted for you,' Spencer said, positively beaming at them. 'You're a very lucky man, Jannes. But I do hope this doesn't mean you're changing your plans for the Transat.'

'Oh, no. Trust me, nothing is going to change on that front.'

'Well, good,' Spencer said. 'Because I've decided—I'm in. I already spoke with your agent, but I wanted to let you know in person.

Now I've met you—and you, Lara—I see that you're exactly the kind of person I want my business associated with. Now, I won't keep you any longer as I believe you have some very important shopping to do.'

Lara made polite goodbyes and Jannes shook Spencer's hand, not quite sure whether he was more in shock about the sponsorship or the fact that he'd suddenly found himself engaged to Lara.

They sat in silence for a few moments, watching Spencer leave.

'Jannes, what the he—?'

He returned her stare, eyebrows high. 'Mormor,' he said. 'She must have done this.'

'Why?' Lara spluttered. 'That's completely— You don't just announce someone else's engagement without even speaking to them about it. Especially when they're *not actually engaged.*'

'She's calling our bluff,' Jannes said thoughtfully.

'What bluff? We explicitly told her that we're not together. She's the one person on the entire planet who actually had all the information about what was going on with us.'

Jannes shrugged. He couldn't pretend to

understand what Mormor thought she was playing at. 'Maybe she thinks this will make it harder for us to deny there's something really going on between us.'

And maybe she had an endgame of her own in mind. Because, as much as this was a completely bizarre turn of events, Mormor had been right in a way. He had been prepared to let this pretence with Lara fizzle out. Anyone could see that it had been a bad idea to torch the very careful barriers they'd erected between them right from the very start of their friendship.

'So I guess we need a ring,' Lara said at last. 'Need to stick to our story.'

'Lara, you don't have to do this.'

'You've helped me out. All the family stuff... And it's not like we have much of a choice now. Spencer thinks we're engaged. It'll put your sponsorship at risk if we change our story now. You heard him. I'm part of your squeaky-clean image.'

'Last night...' Jannes started, and she wasn't sure where that sentence was going but there was only one thing that they needed to say about what had happened, so she cut him off before he could hurt her.

'We need to forget last night,' she said. 'It was a mistake.'

'Well. That stings.' Jannes looked startled, which he had no right to, considering they'd agreed all along that this was only for show.

'You disagree?' she asked.

'No,' Jannes said quickly. 'Yes. I know we shouldn't do it again. I know that if we give in to those feelings we're going to end up hurting each other. And I don't want that to happen. But I… I don't take it back either. I don't want to pretend that I didn't have those feelings. I love you and I respect you, and it doesn't feel right to lie to you and pretend that I don't feel the way I do.'

Lara looked at him for a long moment.

'Okay,' she said at last, her shoulders set in a straight line. 'You're right; it wasn't a mistake. But it was a complication. One that we can't afford to repeat.'

Jannes nodded, and Lara breathed out a sigh of relief. 'So, do we go ring shopping?' he asked.

Lara slumped back in her chair. 'What on earth was Mormor thinking?'

'That she knows what we want better than we do.'

'You're going to deal with this, aren't you?' she said hopefully. 'Please? Because we cannot have any more curveballs like this. We need to be in control of this.'

Jannes nodded. 'I'll talk to her. I promise. No more curveballs.'

'Then I guess we're going ring shopping. But this time we need to put an expiry date on what we're doing. Because Mormor has just complicated things exponentially. Letting a vague dating thing fizzle out is one thing. That's not going to work once everyone is expecting us to be making wedding plans. We need an exit strategy that works for the both of us.'

He nodded. 'You're right. So we tell people we're not making any plans until I'm back from the Transat.'

She felt a twist of anxiety in her gut, and spoke without thinking. 'In case you change your mind about me?'

'Christ, Lara.' She could see from the expression on Jannes's face that she'd hurt him, that she'd said the worst possible thing. But she hadn't really *thought* it; asking had been a protective instinct, one that she couldn't shake. 'Is that really what you think of me?' he asked. 'Why would you say something like that?'

She shook her head. 'I don't know. Just, I wouldn't be the first girl you changed your mind about while you were racing. I'm… I'm sorry. I shouldn't have said that.'

'No. Get it all out. Tell me what you really think of me. Better to hear it all now.'

'I didn't mean anything by it,' she tried to lie. 'It just came out.'

Jannes shook his head. 'That's not true. You meant that you can't trust me. That you think I'm the kind of person the papers paint me as. That you find their version of me more believable than the person you've known for the last three years.'

She laid her hand on his arm, which was tense under her fingers.

'Jannes, I'm sorry. I was trying to be self-deprecating and I screwed up. I didn't mean to hurt you.'

He shook his head, twitched his arm from under her hand. 'I can't believe you think I'd do that, even to a fake engagement. Like you weren't the most important—'

He cut himself off, and she thought that that was probably for the best.

'It's just that…it's not like I'm not easy to leave, is it? It was a terrible joke about the terrible men in my life who have found me all too easy to disappoint.'

Jannes's hand came up to cup her jaw and she drew in a sharp breath, the feel of his calloused hands on her soft skin sparking a hundred memories of the night before.

'Lara. No one should treat you like that. I'm sorry that you could even joke about that. You deserve better. So much better. Which is why I won't let myself hurt you.'

She met his gaze and held it for a moment, before leaning back and breaking the contact.

'Come on,' Lara said. 'We should go buy a ring if we're going to go through with this.'

CHAPTER ELEVEN

JANNES WALKED BESIDE Lara down the main
street of the town, his hair damp from the
sea mist that had rolled in that morning. They
drew to a halt outside a jewellery store on the
corner of one of the side streets and looked
at the diamonds sparkling under the bright
spotlights.

He glanced across at Lara. 'What do you
think?' he asked, looking along the rows of
ice-white diamonds. Lara's forehead was fur-
rowed, a line appearing between her eyebrows.

'This isn't really me,' she said, and Jannes
nodded. He couldn't argue with that.

'I spotted this place yesterday,' Lara said,
linking her arm through his and leading them
further down the road. She pulled him into a
vintage store he had somehow never noticed,
and they both gravitated to the glass case of
jewellery in the corner by the window.

He sneaked a look at Lara, and saw a quiet smile turning up the corner of her lips.

'This more like it?' he asked.

'Yeah. Much more like…me,' she said.

'Am I a terrible fiancé for making you choose your own engagement ring?' he asked.

She bumped his hip with hers. 'As far as I'm concerned it makes you an excellent fiancé. Imagine having to wear something the rest of your life that you didn't get to choose yourself.'

In the end she chose a vintage opal, milky white with flashes of colour, set in old yellow gold. It was warm and full of character.

'Do you want to wear it now or do you want it in a box?' the shop owner asked them, snipping the thread of the price tag as Jannes handed over his credit card. Lara looked up at Jannes, a question in her eyes.

'Up to you,' Jannes said.

'Then I definitely want to wear it,' she said, holding out her left hand. Jannes felt a surge of possessiveness that he absolutely was not entitled to as he slipped the ring onto her wedding finger.

'It looks good on you,' he said, and before he knew what he was doing his fingers were brushing the nape of her neck and he was touching a gentle kiss to her lips and then to her knuckles. It was just to make their story look real, he told himself as he was doing it. If anyone was to approach the owner of the store about them buying their engagement ring, he would have no reason to think that this was more an arrangement than a relationship.

The owner cleared his throat, and Jannes realised that they were still staring at each other, their lips just an inch apart. Lara caught her bottom lip between her teeth and then turned away from him and turned to the owner of the store with a beaming smile.

'Thank you so much. I love it.'

'Well, I do like to see people fall in love,' the owner said, giving Lara a wink. 'I actually follow you on Instagram,' he continued. 'I just adore your feed.'

Lara fixed him with a radiant smile that almost made Jannes feel jealous.

'That's so nice of you to say. I'm going to follow you right back.' And she pulled her phone from the back pocket of her shorts as she was speaking. Three taps later and she turned the phone to him. 'There. Done. I'm going to tag you as soon as we make an announcement on there. But we're off the grid for the weekend...'

'Of course you are,' he said, smiling at them both. 'Now go celebrate that ring. Champagne all round.'

'Join us?' Lara asked, and Jannes had to suppress a laugh at the irrepressible way that she made friends.

'If I had someone to mind the shop I'd be there,' he said. 'But you'll just have to have one for me.'

After Lara had hugged him and snapped pictures of some pieces she wanted to feature on her feed, and had negotiated hard on the price of a pair of vintage platform sandals, they finally made it out of the store.

'Shopping with you is quite the experience,' Jannes said as they walked back on the main street. 'I never asked you how work is going.'

'It's going well,' Lara said, seizing on the safe topic of conversation and running with it. 'I've been doing some training so I can open my own social media consultancy. There's only so many brands I can partner with, but if I can train others to do what I've done, I can help more people to grow their businesses.'

'Sounds like an interesting pivot.'

She smiled. 'Well, I'm not going to stop what I'm already doing. I love the community that I've made too much for that. Actually, we probably need to talk about that. It's going to look weird if I don't post anything about the engagement. Do you mind if I post a picture of the ring?'

'You're doing it to save my sponsorship,' Jannes said. 'Of course I don't mind. I'm grateful.'

'No time like the present then,' Lara said, positioning them so that the sea was at their backs and pulling Jannes in for a kiss, her left hand up to his face so that it was facing the camera lens. He glanced at the screen when she was done, at the ring catching the light where her knuckles rested on Jannes's cheekbone, sunlight flaring at the side of the frame. Something inside him ached with wanting it to be real. They looked so happy, so right together, that he had to remind himself that it was all for show. That he could never really have the fairy tale that they were presenting to the world.

'You know,' Jannes said as they got back to his house, 'we never had a chance to talk about why you even agreed to go along with this engagement charade. I don't want to make you change your mind but I feel like I should be asking why.'

'Was I not supposed to?' Lara asked, tossing her tote back to one side as they walked through the house, heading for the deck at the back. 'I thought you wanted me to go along with it. It wasn't like I had much choice under the circumstances. I couldn't really argue with a notice in *The Times* in front of Spencer.'

'I know that,' Jannes said, pulling loungers into the sun and arranging them facing out over the water. 'But now we bought a ring and you're talking about it on your feed—'

Lara frowned, and he didn't think he'd ever seen her do that as much as he had this trip. It didn't take a genius to work out that he was already hurting her, despite every intention not to.

'I can't believe you're having a go at me for going along with it,' she said. 'Did you want me to make things harder for you?'

'Of course I don't,' Jannes said, returning from the fridge with a couple of cold cans of lemonade and sitting on the edge of one of the sun loungers. 'I'm not saying I'm not pleased you're doing it; I'm just saying that I would like to understand why. You're my friend and I guess I'm just...concerned. I don't know.'

Lara collapsed in the lounger next to him, all-out scowling now. 'You're concerned by the fact that I'm doing the thing that you want me to be doing?'

'I'm interested in why you're okay with lying to your family,' Jannes clarified. 'To your community, who you just told me mean so much to you.'

'I told you why. You would have lost your sponsorship. I didn't want that on my conscience.' She crossed her arms, and he knew he was pissing her off. He knew equally that this was a conversation they absolutely had to have.

'It wouldn't have been your fault,' he told her. She didn't have to take responsibility for his failings, as much as he was grateful for her help.

'I don't get why you're making a big deal out of this,' Lara said, pulling her sunhat down now so that it hid her features. 'Are you going to start talking about my commitment issues again? Because this looks pretty committed to me.' She flashed him her left hand. She was right; it absolutely did. It looked committed in a way that struck him deep in his bones, making him wish that he had put a ring there for real.

'Maybe we *should* talk about them,' he said gently. 'Because—and I don't know if you know this—most people would find a fake engagement quite extreme, even as a way of helping out a friend.'

'It's convenient,' she said, shrugging, but he wasn't fooled by the casual gesture. 'It will save me a whole load of hassle with my family if I can pretend that we're together. And it doesn't cost us anything—it's not like you even have to turn up to things. But when they try and set me up with cousin Sandra's brother-in-law's son, or whoever it is this time, I just have to play the engaged card.'

He tried to stare her down, but it was impossible with the sunhat and the glasses. She knew what she was doing when it came to avoiding a deep and meaningful talk, he had to give her that. 'Some people might find it a little constraining—especially given what we've said about not doing anything that might undermine our story.'

'But it's not—it's the opposite.' Lara took off her sunglasses and finally looked him in the eye. 'We both know where we stand. We have all our cards on the table. Neither of us can do anything to hurt the other because we both know it's all fake from the start. It's safer, when I know that it's a lie. It's better than something like that taking me by surprise.'

He frowned. 'Because I can't hurt you.'

'Precisely.'

'Because you're not vulnerable,' he pressed.

'Now you're getting it.' She put her glasses back on and looked back over the water.

'But once this is over, pain-free with no surprises, aren't you going to find it hard to be with someone without being vulnerable?'

Lara still refused to look at him, so he knew he was on the right track. 'So I go back to the casual thing I was doing before. No big deal.'

Except she'd told him she was tired of that. And the reason she avoided anything serious wasn't because she didn't want it, but because she was scared of getting hurt.

'This needing the cards on the table thing. Is it to do with your dad?' he asked, knowing that this was sensitive ground.

Lara's gaze was determinedly fixed ahead. 'Why would you ask that?'

'I'm just trying to understand why you settled for this. For me. When you could have so much more.'

'I don't know. Why are you settling for me?'

'I'm not settling.'

He stared at her, knowing he should take those words back, or at least clarify what he meant, but he couldn't. Being with Lara, even temporarily, even pretending, even if he didn't have her for real, could never be settling.

'We should drop this,' Lara said at last, and he could tell from the stiffness of her shoulders that they'd crossed the line and got too close to the truth of what was going on between them.

'So you're going back to London today,' Jannes said, and then bristled at his own words. It sounded too much as if he was trying to get rid of her. 'I think I should come too. I need to talk to Mormor.'

Lara laughed, and he was relieved at the familiar sound. 'Because that worked so well the last time that we tried it.'

His eyes crinkled into a smile. 'She doubled down so I guess now I have to as well. You don't have to come with me.'

'Oh, no, I have a few things I want to say to Mormor.'

'Excellent. More fireworks.'

Lara drove them back to London—it seemed stupid to take two cars—and he'd deal with how to get back to Harbourside later. With her eyes fixed on the road in the exodus of cars following the regatta, he could sneak glances across at her.

'What?' she asked, her eyes never leaving the road.

'*What* what?'

'Why do you keep looking at me?'

He could lie, but what would be the point when she could so clearly read him like a book?

'Just reflecting on how strange this is. How we got here.'

'Bad life choices, I suppose,' she said with a wry grin. 'And Mormor,' she added, with a glance at the ring on her finger.

'Bad life choices and my Swedish grandmother. I wonder how many other people out there can so accurately pinpoint the source of all their problems.'

'I think mine could be summed up as "daddy issues",' Lara said. 'I hate being a cliché.'

Jannes nodded. It was hard not to agree with that. 'We should probably have a lot of therapy.'

'Probably,' she said, but the humour had gone from her voice.

'Hey.' Jannes reached over, his hand just brushing over hers where it rested on the gear stick before she pulled it away. 'I'm sorry. Too far?'

'No, it's fine. I just think you're probably right.'

'I am?'

She nodded, her lip caught between her teeth, her eyes fixed ahead. 'I don't know, but I'm pretty angry, and some of the things you said maybe make me wonder if I'm letting that old cheating, lying bastard have more influence over my decisions than he deserves.'

'Decisions like agreeing to this?' He gestured between them and noted her knuckles were white on the steering wheel.

'Possibly.'

'Well, you know I support you, don't you? I always will.'

Lara glanced over at him and gave him a smile he couldn't quite interpret. 'I know. Maybe we should go together. Is fake couple therapy a thing?'

'I think it's best to keep to one set of daddy issues per session.'

She gave a wicked smile that for some reason set him on edge. 'So we *are* going to talk about how being sent to boarding school at seven is at the root of your commitment issues.'

He shook his head. 'Nope, we definitely aren't going to talk about that.' He threw her a sharp look. 'What could have given you that idea?'

'So it's just me who has to do the soul-searching? God forbid we both work through our issues so we can form healthy adult relationships.'

'Hey, maybe we should save this conversation for when we've had a screaming row with my grandmother,' Jannes said, letting his head fall back against the headrest.

'She scares you.'

'She doesn't scare me; she's just…immovable. It's exhausting.'

'Exhausting and immovable. I can't imagine how difficult that must be for you,' she said pointedly.

He rolled his eyes at the sarcasm in her voice, but had to concede that she had a point. He couldn't support her decision to get therapy without thinking that he probably needed a healthy dose of it himself. It wasn't right that he'd torched every relationship that he had been in. It was one thing not to want a romantic relationship. It was another to want one as desperately as he wanted Lara, and be certain that he couldn't even try without hurting her.

CHAPTER TWELVE

LARA REACHED ACROSS and squeezed his hand as they climbed the steps to Mormor's apartment building. 'Remember,' she said, 'she can't actually force us to get married.'

Jannes nodded, and she recognised the tensing of the muscles in his game face. 'We go in there, explain that she's out of line. She's gone too far and she has to stop interfering in our lives like this.'

'Right. And then we run away.'

He laughed. A little weakly. 'I wouldn't blame you. This thing has got entirely too weird. You had no idea what you were signing up for.'

Lara shook her head. 'I knew I was signing up for you. Mormor's a part of that. Now.' She squeezed his hand again before letting it drop. 'Let's do this.'

But, before they had a chance to knock, the door flew open in front of them.

'Ah, there you are, *älskling*. I wondered when you would get here.' She pulled Jannes in by the elbow and planted a kiss on his cheek.

'We didn't tell you we were coming.'

'I announced your engagement in *The Times* without telling you. Of course you were coming.'

Jannes rolled his eyes. 'So you're not even going to deny it?'

She looked amazed. 'Why would I deny it? It was a stroke of brilliance. I'm rather proud of it.'

'It was manipulative and inappropriate—' Jannes started.

'And yet Lara seems to be wearing an engagement ring.' Mormor interrupted him with a pointed look. 'So it can't have been that terrible an idea.'

Lara could see a muscle twitching in Jannes's jaw as he struggled to keep calm. 'We found out in a business meeting. You didn't give us a choice but to play along.'

'Oh, we always have a choice, *älskling*,' Mormor said, walking down the hallway to the kitchen and speaking to them over her shoulder as she went. 'And you two chose to be engaged. So, congratulations. I'm sure that you're going to be very happy.'

Jannes leaned in the doorway of the kitchen while Mormor bustled around, making them all a drink. Lara looked from grandmother to grandson, amused by the clash of wills, or she would have been amused if she had been an innocent bystander rather than caught up in Mormor's little scheme. 'Mormor, you do know that the ring isn't legally binding, yes? We're going to break this off when the timing is right.'

She threw her hands in the air, and Jannes grabbed for the milk jug she was about to fill. 'Yes, yes, well, you can explain all of that to the vicar if you want.'

'Excuse me, the vicar? What vicar?' Jannes slammed the jug down so hard on the worktop that Lara feared for its safety, but even with the roiling anxiety of the fake engagement it was impossible not to be charmed by the clearly well-rehearsed ballet of Mormor trying to make tea but getting distracted, and Jannes trying to minimise damage but only getting in the way.

'The vicar from the Swedish church, of course,' Mormor said, as if Jannes was the idiot for not knowing which vicar she was talking about. 'Did you know you can't get married in church until you've had the banns read three times? And I told the vicar to start this Sunday, but she absolutely insisted that she had to meet you first. I don't see why she couldn't just take my word for it, as I am your grandmother after all, and why she thinks that she would know better than—'

Jannes came to an absolute standstill. 'Let me get this right,' he said very slowly, choosing his words with care. 'You spoke to the vicar and you tried to have our banns read? Without asking us?'

'Yes, well, if you're going to have the wedding there then you have to book it well in advance.' Mormor carried on setting cups and saucers on a tray, either not noticing or not caring about the storm cloud expression on Jannes's face. 'There's only one Swedish church in the whole of London, you know that. So unless you want this to be one of those depressingly long engagements—'

'But we're not getting married!'

Mormor finally stopped what she was

doing, turned to look at him with narrowed eyes. She fixed Jannes with a look that could make flowers wilt. 'Then why are you engaged?'

Jannes's jaw clenched so hard that Lara worried that he might crack a tooth. She should probably intervene, but there wasn't anything she could say that Jannes hadn't already, and really it was quite amusing, seeing Jannes pushed so close to the breaking point.

'Mormor. We are not engaged,' Jannes ground out. 'We are simply playing along because you've given us no choice. You can cancel the appointment with the vicar—'

'No, well, I can't do that.'

Jannes sighed and pinched the bridge of his nose. 'I don't think I even have the strength to ask why not.'

'Well, because I've told all of my friends at church that you're getting married there. I'd simply be too mortified.'

Which meant that word had probably spread across half the Swedish population of London. Which also meant that trying to deny it would probably spread just as fast, and hit the tabloids before the week was out.

'Mormor, *please.*'

For the first time, the older woman's expression softened, and she reached to cover his hand with hers.

'Look, *älskling*, I've spent a long time watching you be unhappy without saying anything. And now I see how you two are together—' she glanced across at Lara, who felt herself blush '—and I just think, give it a go! I can see how fond you both are of one another. And I know you like to pretend that there are reasons why you can't do this. I'm never going to forgive your parents for the way they treated you. I thought I'd clear the way for you. Show you that it can be that simple if you just decide it's what you both want.'

'But it's not,' Lara said gently, stepping into the kitchen for the first time, and coming to stand beside Jannes. 'We've talked about it, because you're right. We are very fond of each other. But not about the rest of it. I appreciate that you're trying to help, but we don't want this. We're friends, and that's all it's ever going to be.'

Mormor compressed her mouth into a thin line, but didn't argue. 'You'll see I'm right,' she said eventually. 'The appointment with the vicar isn't for a month. I'm not cancelling it.'

Jannes shook his head. 'We won't be needing it.'

'We'll see, won't we?'

'I should be going,' Lara said, looking between them, her heart aching slightly at the way Mormor looked at Jannes, as if he were still a little boy, crying after his parents had left him alone at school.

'I'll let you say goodbye,' Mormor said with a meaningful look before sweeping out of the kitchen.

'So that went…'

'Pretty much as expected,' Jannes finished. 'Don't worry, I'll speak to the vicar. Tell her that Mormor was jumping the gun and we want to wait a bit longer.'

Lara nodded. Then couldn't resist. 'Interesting that Mormor brought up your parents, after what we were talking about in the car.'

'Lara, can we not?' Jannes snapped, and she took a step back, surprised by his tone. 'I'm sorry. But just…not now, okay?'

She wrapped her arms around herself and moved towards the front door.

'Okay, I guess I'll see you next time you're in London then,' she said. 'It's the twins' christening in two weeks. Are you still…?'

'I'll be there.'

'Fine. Great. So I'll see you then.'

She slipped through the front door and leaned against the wall in the corridor, the cool paint soothing against her flushed cheeks. She hadn't imagined that things could fall apart so quickly. She'd never felt closer to another human being than she had to Jannes last night. And now—now she was running away from him because she didn't know how to talk to him any more.

Back in her apartment later that day, she pulled out her planner and looked at her schedule for the week. She was going to have to move things around now that she had an engagement to announce out of nowhere. There were a couple of posts she'd worked on with partner brands that she couldn't move. A post later in the week she'd already bumped twice. If she didn't run it soon she'd end up having to scrap it completely. Which meant that the only good slot for the picture of her engagement ring was…tonight.

She sighed and rested her head on her hand as she scribbled notes to herself. She really wasn't in the mood to come up with a caption that would make sense of her and Jannes's whirlwind romance and sudden engagement. Not least because her online following was based on her authenticity and honesty. When she'd joined Instagram, her shots of London's quiet backstreets, her vintage fashion finds and adventures in upcycling to furnish her flat had only been to entertain her friends.

With her friend Jess as her partner in crime, she'd upped her photography game and spilled her guts in her captions, constitutionally unable to stop herself oversharing. But for some reason it had struck a chord and her followers had gone from the hundreds to the thousands to the hundreds of thousands. Until she'd had enough clout that she'd been able to partner with brands that she loved and turned her hobby into a business.

The thought of lying to her followers turned her stomach. So she started writing, trying to focus on hers and Jannes's friendship and put her feelings for him into words in a way that was truthful.

He was a dear friend. She cared for him deeply. Their relationship *had* changed recently, though not necessarily in the way that people might assume. These were all things that she could say truthfully. As for the 'engagement'…well, she didn't have to say anything, did she. She could just post the picture of the ring and let people make their own conclusions.

It wasn't *honest*, but it wasn't an outright lie either. And she supposed that was the best that she could hope for. She tagged Jannes in the photo—her stomach lurching as she caught sight of his profile picture, that same shot of him they had used at the awards ceremony, a magazine shoot for a menswear brand, with Jannes hanging half off a yacht in a shirt that had once been white but had been rendered transparent by virtue of being dripping wet. She really shouldn't be driven to biting her lip over someone who she was meant to think of as just a friend. She'd been suppressing these thoughts and these feelings for Jannes since the day that she had met him—you'd think that she'd be better at it by now. But her trip to Harbourside, the fireworks, had changed all that, and she wasn't sure how they were meant to get back to normal. Not while they were meant to be engaged.

She hit post, and almost instantly the comments started flooding in, full of love hearts and bride emojis and the occasional aubergine.

She shut down her laptop—normally she interacted as much as she could in the comments, but she couldn't for this post. Even accepting the congratulations would make her stomach twist with guilt. Would make her melancholy for what she couldn't have.

She had never thought that she could lie about something so important. She had spent half her life wondering how that bastard of a father had come home to her and her mother every night—or every night he wasn't with his other family—and now she had some insight. All it needed was high enough emotional stakes, and intense enough feelings, and you found yourself making choices that you couldn't have imagined making just a few weeks before. Was this how it had been for her dad? One choice leading to another to another, until the lies got away from you and you had no choice but to stick to your story or see your life fall apart.

The big difference, of course, was that no one else's feelings were at stake. Everyone who was emotionally invested knew the truth. But Lara's online community was just that—a community. Full of people who she had never met in person but nonetheless considered to be friends. Was she hurting them, by bending the truth about her and Jannes's relationship? Or was it their business and nobody else's what was going on behind closed doors? She didn't even know that *she* understood what was going on. Okay, they had no intention of getting married, that much was clear. But what about the kisses that they'd shared? The night that she'd spent wishing that she was in Jannes's bed instead of her own? That wasn't exactly platonic, was it?

What they were doing in public was acting out what would have been happening in private if it weren't for the scars they were both carrying that made a romance between them impossible. It was an alternate version of her future playing out before her, and her and Jannes were the only ones who knew that she wouldn't be able to keep it.

Her phone rang, and she hesitated when she saw Jannes's name on the screen. She really didn't want to speak to him just now, when her feelings were so jumbled from having written that caption, and then looked at that picture on his profile. But the longer they went without speaking, the more awkward it was going to get. She hit answer and tried for an easy breezy, 'Hey.'

'Hey. My notifications just blew up. Do I take it we're official?'

'As of about five minutes ago. Everything okay at Mormor's?'

He sighed. 'She's singing. Absolutely delighted with herself as far as I can see. Not a smidge of remorse.'

'She's a monster.'

Jannes laughed out loud. 'That might be a little harsh considering all she wants is for us to be happy.'

'Hmm. Are you going back to Harbourside?' she asked, telling herself it was just friendly chitchat rather than her wanting to know how much longer he was going to be in town.

'My agent organised a couple of meetings for me here tomorrow now that Spencer is on board. Then back to Harbourside and a training camp in Norway. I don't know how contactable I'll be...' His voice trailed off and she realised that this was a 'couple' sort of conversation. Checking in and warning of radio silence. Was this where they were with one another now? Explaining your whereabouts like you would with a real-life fiancé?

She felt a familiar twinge of discomfort at this. That they were becoming more to each other than just a lie. This was where she usually started a subtle freak-out. Because when the person she was with started telling her where they were going to be, making plans to see her, she had to decide whether she was going to believe them. Or whether they were just telling her what she needed to hear, covering their tracks so that they could do what they wanted without getting caught. This was the part where trust came in. When it started to matter to her whether the other person was telling the truth. And, invariably, it was where she threw up her walls, ensuring that no one would be able to hurt her.

She had to remind herself that it didn't matter whether Jannes was telling the truth. That their relationship was a pretence. That even if he did lie to her, she wouldn't get hurt because he didn't owe her the truth. He didn't owe her anything. That was what made this safe—a relationship that she *knew* was based on a lie could never hurt her. That was what made this different.

'Well, have fun,' she said, at what she hoped was an appropriate place in the conversation. She didn't want to admit that she'd got distracted wondering whether she should care if he was telling her the truth. By wondering what their relationship might be like if she wasn't so...damaged.

'Are you sure you're okay?' Jannes asked, and she guessed she hadn't pitched her voice quite right, that he'd heard something of her doubts.

'Yeah, I'm sure,' she lied, before hanging up with a rushed goodbye.

CHAPTER THIRTEEN

Two weeks later, and Lara had to conclude that her followers were so in love with Jannes on her behalf that it made up for the fact that they were faking the whole relationship. She'd posted some pictures from early in their friendship, focusing on the truths in their relationship—that shared history—rather than the fictional future that they were meant to be planning. She'd declined all requests to partner or advertise anything wedding-related, pleading for the moment her intention to enjoy her engagement before starting wedding planning. She might be doing something morally dubious in not revealing the full truth about her engagement, but she wasn't so morally bankrupt that she would use her fake engagement to make money.

She concentrated on the coursework for her MBA—life would be so much simpler with a consultancy business, which didn't rely on snapshots of her personal life. Jannes had been away at his training camp in Norway for the past two weeks. And should have been on her doorstep an hour ago to go with her to the twins' christening.

But there was no sign of him. His phone wasn't ringing and her messaging app said he hadn't logged in since yesterday. And every time she thought to herself that she'd throttle him if he made her go to this thing alone after she'd told people that he'd be there, she wondered if it was something worse than him letting her down going on. Whether something had happened to him out on the water. That maybe he wasn't coming back to her at all.

Her stomach gave a lurch of fear. Thinking about how he was letting her down was at least a distraction from worse thoughts. She glanced at the time on her phone. If he wasn't here in the next fifteen minutes then she was going to be late to the church—and showing up solo. This whole thing with Jannes was meant to be sparing her intrusive questions— if she showed up without him after they'd RSVP'd that he would be there it would be bound to prompt faux sympathetic looks and whispers behind her back, entirely defeating the object of this whole charade.

Eventually she fired off a text, letting Jannes know that she was leaving without him. Maybe if he got it in time he would be able to meet her at the church.

She made sure her phone was synced with her car, just in case he called or messaged while she was on the road to the country church. More floral shift dresses and pashminas. More florid uncles backslapping one another in the hotel bar at the reception afterwards.

If they staged another intervention like the last one, she was certain that she would either die or explode with rage. Which didn't really seem fair to them, considering the rage was mainly directed at the man who had screwed over their lives as much as hers.

And, speaking of the devil incarnate, if she wasn't mistaken, she was going to have to spend the afternoon dodging that loser of a sperm donor. Pip hadn't invited him to her wedding, but she knew this branch of the family were still on speaking terms with him. Thinking about her father was more uncomfortable than ever now that she was living her own version of his lie. She didn't want to see what he had done to her in a different light. She'd spent her whole adult life trying to come to terms with the damage that he had done, and thinking of him as human again, rather than a monster, only made things more complicated.

Jannes would have been the perfect person to have her back, to keep her safe—God knew he'd proved as much at Pip's wedding. All of which was an excellent distraction from worrying that something might be seriously wrong.

She had always been slightly ill at ease when Jannes was out at sea and incommunicado. When he was on land they would text a few times a day—just mundane stuff about what they were doing, work, mutual friends. So when her phone went silent, nothing felt quite right until that message pinged letting her know that he was back.

But it had never felt like this before, this gnawing feeling that something must be seriously wrong. If he hadn't just decided that this event—that she—wasn't important enough for him to show up—or even let her know that he could be late. Her hand itched with the urge to check her phone, even though she knew that if he'd called or messaged she would have got a notification on the car's screen. But the anxiety was making her rational brain more annoying than helpful.

As the mileage countdown on her satnav reached single figures, she gripped the steering wheel tighter. So tense that when she reached the church, and Jannes was parked right outside, hands in his pockets and sunlight bouncing off the blinding white cotton of his shirt and the lenses of his sunglasses, she wasn't sure whether to kiss him, hit him or throw up on him.

Relief flooded her body like a drug as she threw open the door of her car and marched across the car park, only stopping when she had two handfuls of Jannes's shirt in her clenched fists.

'Where the hell have you been?' she managed to say through clenched teeth.

'Um...hi to you too?' Jannes said, his voice low and amused as he glanced down at her white-knuckled fingers still grasping at his shirt.

She could barely breathe with the relief of seeing him, and had to force in a breath to be able to yell at him. 'You were meant to be at my place two hours ago!'

'We…have an audience,' he said, looking past her shoulder, and she could imagine the eyes of a couple of dozen relatives fixed on her and Jannes.

They both had parts to play, she remembered. The fact that she didn't even know if she was angry with him or relieved, or delighted, didn't really matter.

'Oh, we should…' She tried to kick her brain into gear, but Jannes was already on the case. His hands came up to cup her cheeks and she shuddered as he dipped his head and pressed his lips to hers. She pulled him closer with the fists still clenched against his chest and it wasn't until she opened her mouth under his that she remembered that they were at a family event. At church.

'I'm so angry with you right now,' she said softly, pulling away though every cell in her body was protesting at the loss of him.

'Funny way of showing it,' Jannes retorted, his hands falling to rest on her hips.

'Yeah, well, we'll talk about that later,' she said, uncurling her fists and grabbing his hand instead. Adrenaline was leaching from her system and she suddenly felt limp, as if she just wanted to lean into him and soak in the fact that he was here and whole. She practically dragged him into the church and down beside her onto a pew.

'I thought you'd been eaten by sharks,' she said, keeping her face deadly serious, although it was tucked firmly into his shoulder, so the effort was probably wasted on him.

'And this is the sympathy I get?'

She glanced at his face to see that a corner of his mouth had quirked up, which only made her more angry. 'I swear, if you get yourself eaten by sharks I'll be furious with you.'

'I'm sorry I worried you,' he said, tucking a piece of hair that had escaped her messy bun behind her ear. Why did he have to be so impossibly reasonable all the time? 'My phone died and I didn't have your number. I didn't have time to get to your apartment so I figured the best thing to do was to meet you here.'

'Your phone died?' she asked him. Why had abandoning her and being eaten by sharks featured higher on her list of possibilities than the more reasonable dead phone explanation?

'Sank, actually. Occupational hazard.'

She shoved at his shoulder with her chin. 'I was *worried*.'

'I know. And I truly am sorry.' He pulled her tighter to him with an arm around her shoulder and kissed the side of her head. 'I'll make sure the whole crew have your number next time, just in case. No more risk of complete radio silence unless I've warned you beforehand. I promise.'

'Good,' Lara replied, relaxing gently against his side. 'Now. How much of an exhibition did we just make of ourselves on consecrated ground?'

He grinned. 'I'd say an appropriate amount for a newly engaged couple who have been separated for a fortnight. Do you want to go and say hi to your family?'

She looked towards the door of the church, but more and more people were coming in, and they'd only be fighting against the flow of people if they tried to leave now.

'No, let's stay here. We'll catch up with people after the ceremony. Tell me about your training camp. How was it?'

She listened as he filled her in on what he had been up to for the last couple of weeks, and she tried to keep her eyes and her mind on him, rather than the people entering the church.

Eventually, she heard a squeal and Pip was climbing over people in the pew behind to try and reach her. She dragged first Lara and then Jannes into a hug, then grabbed Lara's hand to look at her engagement ring. 'Congratulations, you guys!' she said. 'Why didn't you tell us? Another wedding!'

'Oh, we didn't want to steal your thunder,' Lara said, throwing a quick look at Jannes. 'How was your honeymoon?' she asked, looking for a quick change of subject.

'Oh, you know, decadent, idyllic—you'll find out soon enough,' she added with a wink.

She was spared having to think of a reply by the vicar clearing his throat at the front of the church.

'I'll talk to you later,' she whispered to Pip, who hurried back to her seat.

Lara kept her gaze fixed forward throughout the ceremony, resisting the twin urges to look around to see if her father had shown up, or to get her fill of Jannes's face, to assuage that anxious feeling in her belly that persisted even though she knew he was sitting beside her. It wasn't until the adrenaline started to wear off that she realised how worried she had been, and now that he was here beside her it was as if she was finally free to imagine every terrible way she might have lost him. A huge wave of fear and relief hit her at once, and she felt for his fingers with her own, nudged his pinkie and then tangled their fingers together.

In her peripheral vision she saw him glance across at her, worried, then he squeezed her hand and lifted their linked fingers to his lips.

That simple kiss shouldn't have stirred her and stilled her all at once. It should have been either one or the other—the comfort of a friend or the spark of a hook-up. The two together? Well, it was unprecedented, and that meant it couldn't be trusted. That was what she had fought to stay away from all these years, because she knew that it could lead to nothing but heartache.

But also it felt...right. In a way that should have her running from it, while simultaneously making even the thought of doing so completely impossible. Because if she didn't, one or both of them was going to get hurt. But...wasn't that going to happen either way?

Walking away from this wasn't a pain-free option any more. Not after Harbourside. She compromised by pulling her hand back and having it rest in her lap, in a demure fashion she was certain she had never attempted before.

Jannes glanced across at her, but she refused to make eye contact. She should at least try to look as if she was paying attention if she was going to convince Pip and her mother that family therapy wasn't really a thing that she needed because she was perfectly fine and had a perfectly fine boyfriend thank you very much.

The service ended with the twins in tears, the godparents looking traumatised and the vicar shouting valiantly, if not terribly successfully, over the racket. The combination of crying babies and organised religion could hardly be a more perfect storm for guaranteeing that she wanted a drink. She dodged relatives in the churchyard and headed straight for the hotel over the road where the reception was being held. At some point during her manoeuvres for the exit, Jannes must have worried about losing her in the crowd because his hand had found its way back into hers.

She didn't even bother shaking him off. It was easier if they stuck together. That was definitely the reason she let her hand disappear into his palm. Nothing to do with feeling anchored and secure in a situation that would normally make her flighty and adrift. Would normally be sneaking off to her car rather than risk having to make conversation with her father. She'd seen him there in the church, near the back, as if he couldn't be sure of his welcome. And so he should, because she couldn't understand how any of them could even stand to look at him. Some people were sentimental about family, she supposed, congratulating herself for not being one of them.

'Are you thirsty?' Jannes asked as they entered the cooler air of the hotel lobby, the door swishing closed after them, shutting out the sound of the christening party not far behind.

'A tactical retreat,' she said. 'Nothing worse than being ambushed in a churchyard.'

'I'll have to take your word on that one. Your dad?' he added gently. 'Or are the mums worse?'

'Dad. He was at the church. Don't know if he's coming here, but if he does I want to see him before he sees me.' Especially given

the thoughts that she'd been having recently.
The ones where she compared her behaviour
to his and started to realise that he probably
hadn't wanted to hurt her. That her pain over
the years had come from his failings, but not
necessarily his malice. Did it matter, that she
could see more clearly what had happened
now? Should it make a difference to her,
knowing that maybe he had still loved her,
even while he was hurting her? That things
weren't as clear-cut and simple as she had
made them when she was a teenager.

'When was the last time you spoke to him?'
Jannes asked.

She tried to keep her voice matter-of-fact.
'The night we left home and went to live with
Pip and her mum. He tried, for a while, to get
me to speak to him, but he gave up eventually. I'm sure he won't even care that I'm here
today but I don't want to risk it.'

'Okay, well, I'm here. Just tell me what you
need.'

It was only as she squeezed his hand that
she realised that she was still holding it,
though there was no risk of losing one another
here, and no one they were trying to convince they were a couple either. She should

pull away, she knew, keep straight what they were to each other—what was pretence and what was real—but she didn't want to. And Jannes wasn't pulling away either.

'So what's the play if we see him? Offence or defence?' Jannes asked.

She wished she was relaxed enough to feel grateful to him, but she couldn't yet. Couldn't think much beyond the fact that her father was going to be in the same room any minute now, and she hadn't decided what she was going to do when she saw him. 'Which is the one where I down my G&T?'

'Defence, then,' Jannes clarified, scanning the room behind them.

'Keep at least five people between us at all times, please?' Lara said. 'And if you block my view of him with your big manly shoulders then even better.'

'You think my shoulders are big and manly?'

She rolled her eyes. 'Is that really what you're taking away from this conversation?'

'Yes, I'm your distraction, remember? Let me distract you.' She smiled at the way that he always seemed to know how to get through to her. Knew exactly what she needed.

'You're definitely that,' she said. 'Have you spoken to Mormor while you've been away?' It had taken her two weeks to get her head around the last spanner that Mormor had thrown in the works. She needed to know that there weren't going to be any others heading in their direction.

Jannes shook his head. 'No, and I dread to think what she's been up to since I've been gone.'

'Well, you can put "aggressively liking my posts on Instagram" on the list,' Lara said.

'Oh, no, tell me she hasn't. She's never liked one of my posts.'

Lara gave a tight smile. 'Ah, well, you've got a treat ahead of you. Anything remotely regarding the two of us and she is *very* enthusiastic with the emojis.'

'Stop it. No. I can't…' Jannes wheezed, desperately trying to hold in a laugh, the bastard. She could see his shoulders shake, and realised how much she loved that. Making him lose control, even like this. Even when it was pissing her off at the same time.

'Don't say I didn't warn you,' she said with a smug smile.

But then a buzzing started in her ears, and

she lost the sense of what Jannes was saying until his hand cupped her cheek and her eyes snapped back to him.

'Dad alert?' he asked.

'Yes. Just arrived. Get your shoulders over here.'

She pulled him into position so that she was shielded from view for most of the room, and tried to track her dad's progress as he made small talk with various relatives.

'So your mum and Gloria still think you need therapy, huh,' Jannes said quietly, so only she could hear.

'Something like that,' she replied, still peering around his shoulders, trying to keep an eye on her dad without him seeing her.

'And you're resistant to this idea because...' Jannes prompted.

'Because I'm fine.'

He raised an eyebrow. 'Says the woman hiding behind the man she's fake agreed to marry.'

Lara rolled her eyes. 'Family therapy would be worse. They wanted him to be there. They think I need to have it out with him.'

'And do you think that maybe they have a point?'

'I'd rather stick swords in my eyes.'

Someone cleared their throat behind Jannes and she felt ice-cold in her chest.

Jannes made eye contact with her. She knew that if she needed him to, he would stand in front of her, blocking her from view and protecting her in their corner of the bar, even while her dad stood there watching them. But she wouldn't make him ridiculous for her sake. This was her own fault for letting herself get distracted and not seeing him approaching. For forgetting that avoiding her father should have been her number one priority.

'Yes, it's okay,' she said, moving him gently aside with a hand on his chest. 'What do you want?' she said to her father in a low voice, making her face neutral and blank. The only thing worse than having to see him would be showing him how much it hurt. She wouldn't let him think that he *mattered*.

'Hello, Lara. I've missed you so much. Do you think we could go somewhere and...?'

'And what?' she demanded, anger welling up inside her from she didn't know where. 'I don't want to talk to you. I want nothing to do with you.'

'Lara, please, can we just…?'

'No!' she said, and realised too late that she was shouting and didn't seem able to stop. '*You* "just"—just listen to me. I don't want you in my life. Why won't you respect my decision?'

'I'm getting married,' her father said, and she felt something hollow out inside her. Another family. Another try at having a family. She could be replaced, again, just like that. 'I really want you to be there,' he said. 'Or just back in my life, however you want.'

'I'm not interested,' Lara spat, her anger burning hot and white in her chest. 'I pity your fiancée!'

'Lara, please,' he said, his face reddening, a prickle of sweat at his hairline as he glanced over his shoulder at the room. 'I'm your father.'

'No! You're not!' She could feel her control slipping even further, could feel the walls closing in on her and the friendly hum of conversation in the bar became an oppressive buzz in her ears. 'Jannes, let's go.'

She slotted her fingers through his and stalked from the bar, studiously ignoring the stares of her assorted family as she did so. Let them look—she was hardly the one at fault here. That honour went to the feckless excuse for a father that she was currently walking away from. She dragged Jannes away from the front of the hotel, across the car park and through a gate beside the church that led to a small area of woodland.

'Lara? What's going on? Are we digging a g—? *Oh.*'

He stopping speaking as Lara smashed her mouth against his, sliding her hands into his back pockets and dragging him closer. She turned them both, pulling until her back was against a tree, the rough bark biting into her skin between her shoulder blades. But with a gentle hand on her cheek, Jannes eased himself away, looking down at her, panting and flushed.

'Not that this isn't…you know,' he said, a little breathless, pulling her closer by the hips for a second. 'But I'm not sure that being angry at your dad is a good reason to do this.'

'Can't you just shut up and kiss me? It's a lot easier to not think about it when we're doing that.'

Jannes groaned. 'And while it's *extremely*

flattering that you're using me that way, I'm not sure I want to be your human stress ball.'

She leaned away from him, her hands still wedged in his back pockets. 'You're turning me down.'

'I'm not turning you down,' he said, through a jaw so tight she was surprised he could get the words out. 'You don't really want me. You're just working out your issues on me and I think things are complicated enough.'

'None of which would matter if you actually wanted me,' she insisted. Of all the times to turn her down… Normally, she could take it. But now she just needed him to need her as much as she did him. She needed what they had not to be a lie. She needed to not be her father, with a web of complicated relationships confusing the people around her. She loved Jannes, and she needed him to love her back.

'This isn't about wanting,' Jannes said, maddeningly calm in the face of her panic. 'I don't know how you could possibly believe that I don't want you after the last couple of months. This is about us making good choices, for good reasons. I don't think you can know what you want while you're mad at your dad.'

'Well, screw you then, Jannes,' she said, pushing him away. Because if she shoved hard enough, put enough distance between them, she could make herself believe that he couldn't hurt her any more. That the fact that she loved him and he didn't love her back didn't flay her and leave her raw. Her hands came up and she clenched them in front of her chest. Jannes took half a step back and then pulled her to him, her forehead against his chest and her shoulders shaking as he wrapped his arms around them.

'Jannes, no, you can't. You can't make this better. I'm… I'm broken. There's something wrong with me, and as much as I want you— us—to fix it, it isn't going to happen. You should get away from me. I'm going to hurt you if you do this.'

'You're angry. As you have every right to be,' Jannes said, letting his arms fall away as she pulled her shoulders back and sucked in a long breath, her arms crossing back over her body. Her gaze darted past him, back towards the churchyard and the car park. 'But I don't think you're angry at me, and I don't think this is the time to be changing what we are to one another.'

'You drove here, right?' Lara asked. 'You don't need me to give you a ride home.'

'I have my car,' he said, his voice wary. 'You're leaving?'

'I have to. I can't go back in there—I'm not going to humiliate myself any more.'

'And you're leaving without me?' She knew that she was hurting him. Knew that she shouldn't walk away from him. But she needed to be away from here, and she needed to be alone.

'You should stay. It's an open bar. And apparently the buffet is going to be excellent.'

'Lara.' He turned her face up to his. 'You know full well that I don't care about the bloody open bar. I care about you—don't do this.'

She shook her head. She didn't have a choice. 'I'm sorry. I have to go.'

'You're walking away from me.'

She glanced past him, back towards the hotel, the party, her family.

'Yes. I'm sorry.'

And with that she walked past him, and he watched her until he heard the creak of the gate and she disappeared into the trees.

* * *

She texted him later that night, when the adrenaline and anger had deserted her, and she was left feeling limp and uncertain.

I'm sorry. Can we talk?

She watched her phone for an hour, a cup of coffee growing cold beside it, waiting for Jannes's response. She didn't even know where he was—whether he had driven back to London or Harbourside, or straight to the marina and headed out on the water. It was unsettling to feel so adrift just because she didn't know where he was. What they were to each other right now.

How had they messed this up so badly? Because *she* was messed up. She'd fought with her dad, thrown herself at her friend, been rejected, and then walked out on him.

She had messed up in the worst possible way, and she deserved every bit of anger she was sure Jannes must be feeling. She just wished he would show up and be angry in person. Or at least call her and be mad at her on the phone, because this silence was killing her. She just needed to know that they were going to be okay. That they could pretend the last six weeks hadn't happened and go back to being friends who stridently ignored the chemistry between them, because they knew the massive disaster that would ensue if they ever decided to cross that boundary.

She checked her phone again, even though she knew she would have heard it buzz if he'd messaged back. She cycled through her social media apps—turned out someone had shared a picture of them kissing before the christening, when she'd been so relieved to see that he was safe.

And then she remembered that he'd lost his phone, and she'd been waiting for a call that was never going to come. She dropped her head into her hands. What had she done?

CHAPTER FOURTEEN

LARA SNAPPED AWAKE the next morning as a message pinged, sitting up suddenly in bed and scrambling to read it, her hands shaking.

It was from Jannes.

Hey, sorry, just got a new phone. Want to talk now?

She replied before he could change his mind.

Yes. Please. Are you in London?

Maybe she should have worried about looking too eager, but she was desperate and there was no point hiding it.

Yeah. London Fields? Ten?

Meet you in our usual spot.

She showered and dressed quickly, running through conversations and arguments in her head, rehearsing what she could say to bring him back to her. To apologise for the way she had thrown herself at him and then run away when he'd quite understandably turned her down. And before any of that they had to decide what they wanted. What *she* wanted. Because she knew that until she'd done that there was no point talking at all.

Yes, she was angry at her dad. And yes, she had every right to be. But maybe her mum and Pip's mum and Jannes all had a point—maybe she was letting that anger make decisions for her when she should be making them for herself. She'd had more of an insight into her dad's life than she cared for, faking this thing with Jannes, and maybe she hadn't dealt with her feelings about him in the healthiest possible way. Was she going to carry on like that—avoiding the things that she was afraid of, rather than choosing the things that she wanted? How long had her choices really been just a reaction against a man who had lied to her and broken her heart before it was fully formed?

She pulled a comb through her hair and pulled on a floral jumpsuit and her vintage gold sandals. Slipping earrings into her lobes, she hesitated over the gold and opal ring sitting in the jewellery dish on her dresser. Whether she chose to put it on or not sent a message. In the end, she wore it. It was just keeping the status quo, she rationalised to herself, and being photographed without it would be a hassle until she and Jannes had had a chance to talk and decide whether they were keeping this pretence of an engagement going, and if they weren't, how they were going to get out of it.

She slipped the ring onto her finger and breathed out a sigh at the reassuring weight of it over her knuckle. She wouldn't think too much about how attached she was to it already.

Eventually, she would have to. She'd been avoiding thinking about how she was feeling since the day her dad had left her, and maybe that wasn't the right thing to be doing. At some point, maybe she should look a little deeper, at the wounds that she was carrying around, and whether they were affecting the choices that she made.

She didn't have to do it with her family there—she wasn't ready for family therapy yet—but she had been carrying this anger for so long. And it had pushed her to the edge of control, and risked ruining her…whatever it was she and Jannes were…because she couldn't be in the same room as her father.

She pulled the door closed behind her and walked quickly down the sun-dappled pavements to the corner of Broadway Market, where she and Jannes had been meeting for weekend brunches for years. Where she had met him just a few weeks ago and concocted this plan which had soon spiralled way out of her control.

She spotted Jannes before he saw her, and she watched him approach, watched the subtle glances directed his way from men and women alike. He saw her at last, and attempted a smile that turned into a grimace, and she knew that things were very different from the last time that they'd walked here.

'Hi,' she said as he drew close, and one corner of his mouth turned up in a smile that didn't reach his eyes.

'Hey,' he replied, with such a sad tone deep in his voice that she knew she had broken something that couldn't be fixed. Whatever happened next, things could never go back to how they'd been before she had brought him into that glade and acted out her fear and anger and sadness on him, until he'd had no choice but to push her away.

'Do you want to eat or walk?' Jannes asked, and Lara turned towards the park.

'Walk?' she said. She couldn't eat, not the way she felt right now. She'd be sick.

They set out on the path that took a wide circle around the park. It was still quiet this morning, and they didn't have to worry about being overheard.

'You're still wearing the ring,' Jannes said as an opening gambit and she was relieved beyond measure that she had decided to wear it.

'I didn't want to presume...' she started, picking her words in a way she'd never had to with Jannes before. Something between them had broken, and she didn't know how to fix it.

They walked on in silence, and she didn't know where to start trying to reach out to him.

'I'm sorry,' she said at last, because it was

the most important part of what she had to say. 'I shouldn't have walked away from you like that. I knew it would hurt you and I did it anyway and I'm so sorry for that. And I'm sorry for the way that I threw myself at you too. I really messed up, and I want to make it right again.'

'I want that too,' Jannes said, his voice full of regret. 'So much. But I think we're wrong, trying to go back to how we were before. I don't think we can do that. Too much has happened. Too much has changed.'

'But I care about you, Jannes. I really do. Can't we just keep hold of that?'

He wasn't sure if they could. He'd watched Lara walk away from him at the church, and it wasn't until then that he'd realised that it was his every worst nightmare come true. This was exactly why he'd avoided getting involved with her in the first place. They'd thought that they were so clever, with their rationalisations and their fake dating, and their 'just going along with it, nothing to do with us' when Mormor had upped the stakes. And in fact what they'd been doing was walking blindfolded into exactly the situation they had both sworn that they were going to avoid. When she'd hurt him, he'd realised it was exactly what he'd been scared of all along.

'I think we have to stop this,' he said as they reached the end of a path.

'Stop here?' she asked, her forehead wrinkling in confusion.

'No,' he said, turning to face her. 'Stop this—' He gestured to himself, to her. 'I can't pretend to be with you and want to be with you, and then…not be,' he said, feeling his stomach swoop as he admitted how he felt about her.

'You want to be with me?' Of course that was the part she heard, not the breaking up part. She wouldn't be Lara if she'd heard anything else.

'Of course I do,' he said, reaching for her hand, and then reminding himself. 'You must know that. You know what I would want if things were different.'

She shook her head, and he knew that she wasn't going to take being broken up with without a fight—the fact that the whole thing had been fake from the start didn't make a difference to that.

'What things?' Lara asked. 'All we have to

do is decide if we're doing this—if we want it. There's nothing stopping us other than being afraid.'

'Then that's what's stopping me,' Jannes conceded. It didn't make him feel very masculine, to admit that fear. He'd made a career of pushing his limits, conquering his perception of what he thought he could do. How little sleep he could survive with. How long he could spend at sea. How fast he could keep moving. But this? He didn't want this challenge. Not when he knew he had no chance of winning. 'I'm stopping myself because I can't handle getting hurt the way I know that I will,' he told her.

She shook her head, taking off her sunglasses so she could look him properly in the eye. 'Jannes, I'm not going to hurt you. I know why you think that, after I walked away.'

'But you don't know, Lara. Because if you did know how much that hurt me, you would never have done it.' This time, she reached for his hands, both of them, and he had to take a step away.

'I've apologised for that. I want to make it right.'

'But this isn't something that you can make right. Because it's not about what you did; it's about how I reacted. There's something wrong with me, and I've accepted that.'

Her face was suddenly so full of pity that he had to look away. 'You can't believe that, Jannes. Please. There's nothing wrong with you.'

He shook his head. 'There is. I promise you. I felt something physically break when you walked away from me. And I understand why you did it—you were upset and hurting, it was a completely normal way for someone to behave in that situation. I'm not angry with you. But none of that changes how I felt watching you leave.

'There's only so many times I can do that to myself, Lara. And I know what will happen—I know who I am. If I'm scared of you leaving me, I'll leave instead. I won't want to, and I'll tell myself that this time it'll be different, but I'll find excuses to be away longer and longer and eventually just never come home. And it will be everything you've ever feared coming true. Just like yesterday was for me.'

She dragged him over to a bench and sat looking at him until he was uncomfortable under her scrutiny. 'I don't think you'd do that to me,' she said, her voice so sincere that he nearly believed her.

'I know that I will.'

'Well, I know you better than anyone else on this planet and I say that you're wrong. And I'm not saying this because I want to be with you. I'm putting that aside and being completely objective here.'

He had to laugh at that; whether it was true or not, it was a bold claim.

'I appreciate your faith in me, Lara, but you can't know me better than I know myself.'

'I can trust you more than you trust yourself. That much is clear. I already do.'

She folded her arms, and he knew that he wasn't going to persuade her that she was wrong. Well, that was fine. He didn't need to persuade her. A relationship didn't exist without both parties being in it, and he had already decided he was out.

'I'm not negotiating here, Lara. I'm telling you. I'm sorry to be blunt, but I think we both need that. No more fake dating. No more fake engagement.'

'And your sponsorship? Spencer?' Of course her first thought was his career.

'They've already signed the contract; the launch is in a month. They can't take it back now. I'll be a disappointment to them, of course, but that can't be helped.'

Her expression turned hard, determined. 'You are not a disappointment, Jannes,' she said. 'I'm going to the launch. You can pretend to date me or marry me or not to know me, if you want, but I'm going to be there to support you either way.'

'I want us to still be friends,' he said, and Lara nodded, because what else could she do? She didn't want to lose him completely, but she knew that their friendship was never going back to what it had been before. How could it possibly, when her feelings had changed so much?

'I can't not have you in my life, Lara. I can't look at you and wonder what will happen if I mess up. If you want something and I'm not able to give it to you and you walk away again. You mean too much to me to take a risk like that.'

'But think about if it worked, Jannes. I can't promise that it will. We both know that. But just…what if it did? Because I love you—

that's not a secret, and I know that you love me too. But there are all these other ways of loving each other that we've only just begun to explore, and I think that if we were brave, and decided to go for it, there's something really special there. Something that I don't know if we would ever find with anyone else.'

'I'm not saying no because I think I'm going to find something better with someone else.'

'But you are saying no?'

'I'm saying that I feel the same way. But the risks are too great, Lara. These last couple of days with things not being right between us—it's been awful. I don't want to go through that again.'

'So we make a commitment to each other—we promise that, whatever happens, we stay in one another's lives.'

'And what happens when we can't keep our promises?' Jannes asked, his voice gravelly.

She didn't have an answer to that and, honestly, she didn't know whether she was relieved or sad. Because he had made up his mind, that much was clear. And she had only just started to sort through her own issues, the things that had been stopping her from committing. She couldn't solve Jannes's problems as well.

She squeezed his hand for a second, before letting it drop. Just for a minute there, she'd been able to imagine her life if this had all worked out, and it was something shining and brilliant, and now completely out of reach.

CHAPTER FIFTEEN

JANNES SAT ON the deck of his yacht, the water calm as a millpond around him. If there had been even a breath of wind then there would be something for him to do, but still and calm like this, there was nothing to do for now but sit and think.

It was meant to be easier out here: that was why he'd come. He'd thought he would suddenly feel a whole lot better than he had when he'd walked away from Lara in the park at London Fields. But he didn't. He didn't feel better on land. Being on the water didn't help either. Which meant he had only one idea left, and he'd been putting that off for as long as he could.

Even as he was walking up the steps to Mormor's apartment, after she buzzed him in from the street, he knew that he was walking into a nightmare. There was no way she was going to look at his miserable face—and there was no way that his face wasn't miserable, given that that was how he felt—and not tell him that he had made an enormous mistake in letting Lara go. They'd said that they were just going to go back to how they were before. That they'd pretend that the dating thing had never happened. But he couldn't. She couldn't. Too much had changed in the last few weeks.

'*Älskling,*' Mormor said as soon as she answered the door. 'Come in and tell me why you are being so stupid.'

He smiled. This was going to go exactly how he'd expected. But something told him that Mormor's tough love was going to be the only thing that helped.

'So you're not getting married any more,' Mormor said, a cup of black coffee steaming in front of her crossed arms.

He sighed melodramatically, thinking that that might get through to her, and shook his head. 'We were never getting married, Mormor. You know that. We *told* you that. Repeatedly. Don't pretend that you've forgotten.'

She huffed in his face, which was precisely the reaction that he'd expected. 'Of course I haven't forgotten, Jannes. Just because I am in my nineties doesn't mean I am an idiot, you know. Anyone with any sense could see that you and Lara were falling in love and going to get married. It's not my fault if you couldn't.'

'Well, we've broken up,' he said, regretting the air of certainty and finality. 'Real us and fake us. It's all over, so you were wrong.'

Her eyes softened as she passed him a cup of coffee and a cinnamon bun. 'I don't know about that. But come on, tell me why you broke up.'

'We weren't right for each other,' he lied.

'Pfft! You're perfect for one another. Try again.'

'I'll end up hurting her,' he said, which was the truth. But he didn't think that Mormor would accept it.

'Closer. Not true, but closer to what you're really scared about.'

He shook his head, feeling the words—the fear—bubbling up and not able to stop it. 'She'll leave me. Of course she will. Even my own parents would drive away from me twice a year without a backwards glance. I know they never looked back because I watched, every time, to see if they would. Or even glance in a mirror. And they never did. I decided a long time ago that I was never going to let that happen again.'

Mormor laid a hand on his shoulder and made a soothing noise. 'And you think Lara would do that to you?' she asked.

'I know that she wouldn't mean to,' Jannes said, looking down at his clenched hands. 'But eventually the novelty would wear off. We'd fight. She'd walk away. I know how these things go. But what's worse is that I won't be content to wait for it to happen. At the first sign of something being wrong I'll be out of there, and I'll hurt her in the process.'

Mormor looked up, tried to catch his eye, but he kept his eyes down, because he didn't need her to see how far down this sadness went.

'I don't think that you do know everything, *sötnos*. I see how much she loves you.'

'Then I'll hurt her, trying to protect myself,' he argued.

Mormor smiled. 'You know, you can just choose not to do that. I'm not saying it's an easy choice. But you *can* choose it. You just have to decide how brave you want to be. I think you have it in you to make this work.

I think you deserve to be happy with Lara. I think she deserves to be happy with you. But that's not going to happen until you decide to make a change. You have to let go of what your parents did to you and decide that you're going to do better than they did. I know at least one person who would never walk away from you. Who has never thought twice about how important you are. Who knows that you would never, ever hurt her. If you can trust yourself to love me, *älskling*, you can trust yourself to love Lara. She deserves it. And you deserve to be happy.'

'I think I need to go for a walk.'

He headed out of the apartment with no idea where he was going, only that he needed to be moving to think about what his grandmother had said. She was right—he'd loved his grandmother since before he could remember, and he'd never once wondered whether she loved him back. Whether it was safe to love her. So whatever damage his parents had done when they'd dumped him in that school, it hadn't touched every part of him. There was a part of his heart that was still undamaged, and he wondered if he knew how to find it. To tap into it. To make it grow.

Because that was what he wanted—he had to admit that now, if nothing else. They might not be able to make it work, but he wanted Lara in his heart. Or wanted to give her more of it, because he really was as stupid as Mormor liked to tell him he was if he thought that she didn't have a place in there already. He'd loved her as a friend for three years, and in that time he had never doubted that she shared his feelings, that she wouldn't want to hurt him. So why did he think that would change if the way that they loved each other changed? Either he trusted her, or he didn't. He trusted himself to be there for her, or he didn't. And if he couldn't trust himself to do those things in a romantic relationship, then he had no right claiming a place in her life at all. Because she deserved better than that.

She deserved someone who would love her wholly, and he did.

He loved her, he trusted her, and he trusted himself to always feel that way.

He half sprinted back to Mormor's apartment with this revelation, a new fear sinking in.

'I don't know if she'll even take me back,' he said, the minute that he was through the door.

'And I can't promise that she will,' Mormor said, waiting for him as if she already knew this was exactly where their earlier conversation had been leading. 'Only you two can work this out. But I can promise you that she loves you. Any old fool can see that much. And I can promise you that, however it goes, I will still be here for you.'

He wrapped his arms around her and rested his chin on the top of her head.

'Thank you, Mormor. I don't know what I'd do without you.'

'You'd do fine,' she answered from somewhere below his chin. 'And you will do, when I'm not here any more to look out for you. But I'd be a lot happier knowing that you had someone else who loves you and trusts you as much as I do.'

He smiled over the top of her head. 'How do I do it? Any ideas?'

'Oh, *älskling*,' she said with a sigh. 'You know her the best. What does she like? What's important to her?'

Well, he knew the answer to that, of course. Her community, the friends and family she had made for herself, when she couldn't rely on one of the people who should always have her back.

'I follow her on Instagram, you know,' Mormor said.

'I had heard something along those lines.'

'And she follows me back. So if there was something that you wanted to say, if there was a grand gesture you wanted to make, for instance…'

But he was already ahead of her, thinking about how quickly he could make it happen, how many people he would have to contact to make it work. He opened his app and checked Lara's account. Okay. A lot. But he could do it, he was sure. He wasn't giving up on her, or on himself. It was time to bring out the big guns.

He pulled up the software that he'd seen Lara use sometimes. Downloaded the picture of them with her engagement ring from the regatta and set to work.

An hour later his hands were hurting from the copying and pasting, and he had a complicated spreadsheet on the go, logging responses from everyone that Lara followed from her feed. If he was going to take it over completely, he needed buy-in from every single person that she followed. Anything other than perfect just wasn't going to fly here. He'd colour-coded everyone's responses, and as soon as he got to the bottom of the list he circled back to the top, making a note of time zones and response time to chase most effectively.

Finally he was *doing* something. He didn't know if it would work. Even if it did, he couldn't be sure that Lara would have him back, but he was finally ready to be brave and he just had to hope that it wasn't going to be too late. He would find out soon enough. This was a one shot deal.

CHAPTER SIXTEEN

LARA SAT AT her keyboard a week later, hoping for inspiration to strike. She'd just spent an hour on the phone with Jess, hoping that it would lift her out of this funk that was leaving her unable to think of a single word to say to the friends she had made online.

Jess was still determinedly in the honeymoon phase, and as much as she had sympathised with Lara over Jannes, there had been no way to keep the treacly sound of happiness out of her voice. And Lara knew precisely what, or who, had put it there. She could hardly begrudge Jess her happiness; it was everything she wanted for her friend and more. But she couldn't help but think that she'd be able to enjoy it with her friend more if her own recent attempts at having a love life hadn't turned out quite so dismally.

She turned back to her scheduling, tried

moving some posts around to see if it helped inspiration strike. But since she'd stopped lying to her followers, and Jannes had disappeared from her feed, she found that she had little to say. Not when she couldn't share her heartbreak with her followers. It was easier to concentrate on her studying, on her consulting clients, anything to take her mind off her own life.

They'd done their best to keep their breakup quiet, trying to avoid the publicity that had prompted the fake dating in the first place, and led to everything that had come after. But that was only viable for so long. It had been over a week now since she and Jannes had been in public together. And though she couldn't bring herself to take off the ring they had picked out together, every time she saw it, it made her just a little sadder that they hadn't been brave enough or bold enough to make this work.

When she closed her eyes she could smell the woodland glade where it had all gone wrong. Could feel the speckled sunlight on her closed eyelids, feel Jannes's shirt beneath her hands and her mouth hard on his. And when she opened her eyes, and knew that it was all an impossibility, it hurt more every time. She'd thought that it would be getting better, that she would be learning to live with this hole in her chest. But it wasn't.

And she knew better now than to think that those sort of emotional wounds just healed themselves. Which was why she'd finally agreed to a session of family therapy, just with her mum to start with. Perhaps she'd work with the rest of the family in future too, but she figured that her and her mum, and the spectre of her dad, had quite enough work to be going on with. The therapist had been really quite insistent that it wasn't her fault that her father had left. Which, intellectually, Lara was sure that she already knew. It turned out it was harder to believe it than to know it. But she was working on that.

She turned to her feed, scrolling through, hoping to find some solace or inspiration in the posts of one of her followers. She'd so often drawn comfort from the community on here. But as she scrolled she frowned and drew back, because something was wrong. Every post was the same—and it was one of hers. The shot of her with Jannes in Harbour-side, showing off her engagement ring for the first time. Had *she* done this somehow? She checked her profile, but no. It had been weeks since she'd posted that picture, and there were plenty of posts since. She clicked back onto the main feed and opened the caption.

Just a hashtag.

#Janneslovesyou

Okay, that was weird. She clicked the next post. The same hashtag. Oh, this had Mormor's fingerprints all over it. It had to be her. She was up to something and she was the only person she knew who could wreak this sort of mischief. She searched for her profile and—surprise, surprise—she found the same post.

Her hands shaking, she clicked through to Jannes's profile and found the same picture, but this one had a caption.

I love you, I need you, I want to marry you. Come to church with me tomorrow?

She closed the laptop, drawing in a shaky breath. Her first guess had been that this was Mormor's doing. Was this him...trying to win her back? For real, or just for some publicity thing? She couldn't get her thoughts straight. Was that what *she* wanted? She had thrown herself at him twice now, and had had to recover from the fallout of him turning her down. Was she really going to put herself out there only to get knocked back again?

No. She couldn't let herself think like that. Couldn't let herself hope, because she was only going to end up disappointed.

But she had been doing the work, hadn't she? She had been to therapy and heard that everything that she told herself about herself was flawed. That the people who had hurt her had made her scared, and she had spent her whole adult life letting that fear win. Well, she had a choice now, didn't she? She could let fear win again, like Jannes had, she recognised, when he had pushed her away. Or she could accept that they were both imperfect and still learning, and still in love with each other, and see what happened when they were both brave at the same time.

She texted him, because the things that she had to say to him didn't belong in church.

I saw your messages. I think we need to talk. My place? An hour?

I'll be there.

She glanced at the clock. She couldn't decide whether that was going to go by in a heartbeat or an eternity. She decided to throw herself into the shower and worry about it from there.

The last time she'd seen Jannes, he'd been walking away from her in London Fields. Walking away because he was afraid that she would leave him. Because he couldn't trust that someone could love him enough to stay. What had changed in the last week? she wondered. Had anything? Because if this was just because he missed her, and not because he had realised that they needed to do things differently, then it was all going to end in tears.

She was never going to find out, though, if she didn't talk to him.

She mused it over in the shower, wondering how he had managed to make sure that she'd seen those posts. It was only when she got out of the shower and checked her feed again, scrolling and scrolling and scrolling, that she realised what he had done. Every single person. He had managed to get every single person that she followed to post that picture of them, of that moment when they had been so happy, so excited, those emotions real, even under the falsities that surrounded them.

They couldn't just keep taking it in turns to freak out and run away each time that one of them had a breakthrough—eventually one of them was going to have to break the pattern so that they could talk about this—that was the only way it could ever work. And Jannes had hit the ball straight into her court. He knew how she felt about him. She'd *told* him how she felt about him.

Her heart stuttered when the doorbell rang, and she knew that this was her last chance to back out. She could carry on being afraid. She could pretend that she hadn't heard the door, hide in her bedroom and wait for Jannes to go away. Or she could be brave, and go out there and talk to him, as she had been desperate to do for the last week.

She opened the door.

Jannes was standing there with his hands in his pockets, looking every inch the poster boy for wholesome Nordic health that he should be.

'Hey,' he said with a hopeful smile, and she reached out a hand and pulled him into the apartment.

'You're here,' she said.

'Yeah, I mean you texted me and… I can go.'

'Don't go, come in,' she said, leading him through to the kitchen, wondering how things could be so awkward when they'd been friends for so long. 'How did you do that to my feed?' she asked, sticking with professional curiosity because that seemed like the safest of all the questions buzzing around her head right now. 'Did you befriend a computer hacker? Break into the algorithm? Because if you did I want your superpowers.'

'No,' Jannes said with a laugh that sounded a little forced. Good, so she wasn't the only nervous one here. 'It was a little less hi tech than that. I befriended everyone that you follow. It wasn't hard, to be honest. They all love you, were happy to do anything I asked if it was for you.'

'But that's hundreds of people,' Lara said, her mouth falling open.

'A little over a thousand, actually. But, like I said, they were happy to do it.'

'I can't believe you did that,' she said, shaking her head, still trying to avoid looking at the big picture, because—frankly—it scared the bejesus out of her.

'Lara, I would do anything for you. I thought you knew that.' Okay, so that was the big picture. Harder to avoid it now that he had said it out loud.

'Last time we talked,' she started, cringing at the memory. 'I asked you... Well, we both know how that conversation went. I put myself out there and...'

'I'm not proud of that. I wish I could go back and change it.'

Lara shook her head. 'But you shouldn't. I've had time to think and I'm sure you were right. I walked away and I hurt you. And I'm working on my own stuff, I even went to therapy with Mum, but the things you said were right—we both hurt each other, and if we try this again we'll end up making the same mistakes and it's not worth losing you over. This last week... God, I've *missed* you, Jannes. So much. And I can't bear the thought that we might do something that means I spend the whole of the rest of my life feeling like that. I mean, marriage! We messed up fake dating. How are we meant to make a real relationship work?'

'We will get things wrong. We'll make mistakes, and we'll argue. But that doesn't have to break us. People make mistakes all the time, and then they apologise and they talk and they figure things out. I know that you love me. And you should know that I love you. I love you a lot. So much, Lara. I want us to take a risk, if it means that we can be happy together.'

'You love me?' she asked, her mind sticking on those three words. 'Even though I don't know if I can do this?'

'Even though you don't know if you can do this,' Jannes said, reaching for her hand, threading their fingers together. 'If anything, that makes me want it more. And even if we decide that it's too big a risk, it's not going to change how I feel about you. You can knock me back and know that you'll still have me in your life. You won't lose me if you don't feel the same way. It's not all or nothing—I'm not giving you an ultimatum. I just want you to know how I feel. That I'm here, offering you my heart, everything, if you decide that that's what you want too.'

'Of course it's what I want,' she said, not able to resist the grin that was spreading across her face. 'It's what I've always wanted. I was just too scared before.'

'Then we're doing this?' Jannes asked.

Lara lifted her shoulders and let them drop. 'I don't even know what this is. Is *this* getting married? Because that still feels like a bit of a leap.'

Jannes shrugged. 'I'm ready to leap. I'm at least ready to talk to the vicar about leaping. But you don't have to be just because I am. We can take this as slow as you want to, or as fast as I want to. We will work out what we need together.'

He pulled her closer with their linked fingers and let his hands fall gently on her hips. She took that as the invitation she hoped it was intended as, and took a step closer until her body was warming against his and she had to tip her head up to see his expression.

'Jannes?'

'Lara?'

'Are you asking me to marry you?'

Creases appeared at the corners of his eyes,

and she wanted to kiss every one of them. 'I thought I had already done that,' he said.

'Not properly.'

One corner of his mouth quirked, and she knew that he was suppressing a smile.

'Well, then.' He took her left hand in his and slid off the gold and opal ring, before dropping to one knee.

'Lara, you're already my best friend, and the person I love most in the world. I was wondering if you'd also do me the honour of being my wife.'

She kept her smile small, not wanting to make this too easy, not after all they'd been through to get to this moment. She wanted to make it last. Leaning down, she brushed a kiss against Jannes's lips, but drew away when his hands came to her hair, before he could deepen the kiss.

'I think that sounds like everything I've ever hoped for,' she said at last, her voice barely more than a whisper, Jannes close enough that it didn't matter.

'That's a yes?'

'Of course it's a yes.'

Jannes's arms clamped around her hips as he stood and spun her around; her dress caught on his jeans as he lowered her, so that her mouth was level with his, her legs locked around his waist. 'You really mean it?' he asked between kisses, as they stumbled their way back onto the couch, Jannes landing on her so heavily that it knocked the air from her chest.

'I really mean it,' she said, one hand on his cheek. 'I love you, I'm going to marry you, and you're going to be mine for ever.'

* * * * *

If you enjoyed this story,
check out these other great reads from
Ellie Darkins

Snowbound at the Manor
Reunited by the Tycoon's Twins
Falling Again for Her Island Fling
Surprise Baby for the Heir

All available now!